"I BELIEVE MY LIFE IS IN DANGER."

"I think my death will be made to look like either an accident or suicide."

Ed made no effort to respond immediately, but let the silence hold while he appraised the fierceness in her blue eyes and the little smirk at the corners of her mouth that was a definite challenge.

"All right, Miss Riff. I am listening, and I'm taking what you say seriously. Since you have come to me with this conviction of personal danger, I assume you have some action in mind that you would like taken."

"No. There is nothing you can do. Nothing can be done before the fact."

Also by Olive Jackson:

AFTERMATH

PROOF OF INNOCENCE

OLIVE JACKSON

Book Margins, Inc.

A BMI Edition

Published by special arrangement with Dorchester Publishing

Printed in the United States of America.

PROOF OF
INNOCENCE

1

Here in her home town where it all began, Renata Riff felt free to walk about alone. She felt no sense of fear that, glancing up, she would see Tanner's detested figure, and be forced to run again. It couldn't last, but for now, freedom was hers to enjoy.

She had taken a heavy jacket from the closet beneath the stairs, shrugged into it, and returned to the foyer of the old Riff house before she realized she must tell the group of four in the living room not to wait dinner for her.

In the middle of framing a speech that would satisfy her brother, Adolf, Renata's thought processes stopped. She could feel a cold draft of fear across the back of her neck. Danger? Her inner voice, well educated in sudden terror, whispered: *danger*.

From somewhere came a low groaning sound. From where? From above! Renata looked up, feeling her eyes grow large and round as she screamed. Above her, the huge wrought-iron chandelier that had hung in the foyer for a hundred years suddenly tilted tipsily, its chains clanging against its wrought-iron bands. For a paralyzing moment the mammoth ornament swayed, then with a hollow, ghoulish sigh, it relinquished its hold on the ceiling twenty feet above and plunged downward. Renata stood directly beneath it.

The Port Haven, California, County Buildings occupied a square block on the western edge of the business district, the main structure fronting on Presidio Boulevard. Renata found ample street parking available when she pulled up in front of the sheriff's wing at nine o'clock on Tuesday morning. For the first time in her life, she entered the desert sand and old rose stucco building through a charmingly arched and recessed doorway. Inside, there was a large waiting area with a few hard benches, and behind a counter, several desks where deputies were busy. At the back of the room two men in plain clothes talked together.

Renata had given her name to the desk sergeant and twice stated that her business was a personal matter she wished to discuss with Captain Ed Staple, before one of the plainclothes men came forward. He was thirtyish, athletic, and moved across the open space with a smooth, silent tread. The desk sergeant looked up at the plainclothes man and smiled.

"Detective Sergeant Mike Wiley," the desk sergeant said, "This is Miss Renata Riff. She wants to see the captain on a personal matter. She says she won't speak with anyone else."

Mike appeared to study the form on which the desk sergeant had written Renata's name and address.

"Riff," Mike murmured, and lifted cool, very clear blue eyes to study Renata. Riff was an old Port Haven name. Mike's smile was easy, with a touch of mischief.

"I'm sure the captain will see Miss Riff," he said. "I'll take her up."

Renata followed up a stair and along an aisle between desks and paused behind Mike while he knocked at an open door at the western end of the building.

"Captain," Mike said, "there's a young lady here says she wants to talk to you and nobody else."

Mike stepped aside and Renata moved unhurriedly into the office, pausing briefly to glance around. The room, if not spacious, wasn't cramped. It was a corner room with two windows, both with old style venetian blinds and no drapes. She had an impression of well ordered efficiency with a minimum of personal memorabilia, except for the obviously antique shelves in the corner between the windows, where a few duck decoys were displayed.

The man behind the desk pushed back his chair and rose to his feet in one easy, fluid motion. He was very physical. Physical, but disciplined, Renata thought, and was uncomfortably aware of her own appearance.

She hadn't expected tailormade clothes, but the easy fit of the navy blue jacket of fine wool hopsacking on shoulders like those could have been achieved in no other way. His pale blue shirt was a fine broadcloth, his tie solid navy, but the vest he wore was a paisley corduroy in which red predominated.

Ed Staple was well over six feet. His brown hair was cut full for a police officer, with an unruly scallop dipping down toward hazel eyes flecked with green. His eyes looked at Renata with a penetrating gaze that was "all seeing," but not unkind. His mouth had an elegant cut with a gentle curve, but his jaw was square and unrelenting.

A complicated man, Renata thought. Would he do? Her glance moved over to the duck decoys and back to Ed's face. Their glances met for a moment before she looked down at her hands. A perceptive type as well, she decided. Yes, he would do. Definitely. She had no doubt that Ed Staple would be a whiz at unraveling tangles.

Ed had looked up sharply from the paperwork on his desk when Det. Mike Wiley knocked at his open door. He had caught the twinkle of mischief in Mike's eye and the smile that had come and gone so quickly. Then Mike had stepped aside revealing a slight female whose proud look had clashed with her mode of dress.

"Captain Staple, this is Miss Renata Riff," Mike said.

Ed took the small hand extended toward him. The hand was calloused. Her face, under the short cropped, sun-streaked blonde hair was a sweetly shaped oval. The small rosy mouth had a sensuous curve. Her threadbare jeans were clean, her nylon windbreaker battered, but the T-shirt underneath the faded plaid cotton shirt was very white.

With a little skin care and a bit of make-up, she would be very attractive, Ed thought. The blue eyes, when he looked into them, looked back with a fierceness that stirred his curiosity and his caution. Her smile came and went quickly as she tipped her head in acknowledgement of the introduction. Ed's instinctive response to her surprised him, and he put a conscious check on the thought that she was trouble.

"Miss Riff," Ed said, "won't you sit down and tell me what I can do for you?"

Mike moved quietly back to take a chair in the corner of the office. Renata gave him a quick look, flashed her smile again, and sat in the chair opposite Ed across the desk.

"Do you know George Kettleman?"

"The bank manager? Yes."

"We're back yard neighbors. His cat introduced us. George said you would listen to me and take what I say seriously."

"We take all citizen complaints seriously, Miss Riff."

Renata's smile flashed again. "Oh, sure." She waved a hand in a dismissing gesture, "only I didn't come to complain."

She looked at Ed intently, deciding whether to go on, he supposed.

"I believe my life is in danger. I think my death will be made to look like either an accident or suicide."

Ed made no effort to respond immediately, but let the silence hold while he appraised the fierceness in the blue eyes and the little smirk at the corners of the mouth that was a definite challenge.

"All right, Miss Riff. I am listening, and I'm taking what you say seriously. Since you have come to me with this conviction of personal danger, I assume you have some action in mind that you would like taken."

"No. There is nothing you can do. Nothing can be done before the fact."

"Has there been a definite threat made against your life?"

"No."

"Who is it you fear, Miss Riff?"

"My step-brother, his wife, and my uncle, Verian Riff."

"Have any of these persons committed an overt action against you indicating they wish you bodily harm?"

"No."

"Then, Miss Riff, what *has* happened to make you believe your life is in danger?"

Renata looked away from Ed, out the window of his office. Her eyes lost their fierceness and took on a far-away look.

"It was Sunday night. I had come down from my bedroom and was standing in the entry. There was a huge old wrought-iron chandelier that hung in the entry . . ."

She paused, her glance returning to meet Ed's.

"It fell. I was standing beneath it and just managed to jump out of the way. One of the chains it hung by hit me across the back. Luckily I was wearing a heavy jacket so it only knocked me down, giving me a few bruises and cuts from flying glass, otherwise I was unhurt."

A chandelier rigged to fall was definitely a hostile act. Inconsistent, Ed thought, not unusual in domestic problems, but. . . . George had sent her. Out of a small silence, Ed said, "You believe the chandelier was made to fall. Is that it, Miss Riff?"

"Not at first, and I'm not at all sure even now. The thing had hung there for perhaps a hundred years; the Riff house was built in the eighteen-sixties. It could simply have given way of its own weight."

"Where were your step-brother and your uncle when the chandelier fell?"

"In the living room with my brother, Adolf."

"Your brother?"

"Yes," Renata said.

"How many people are in the household?"

Renata said, "I should explain, Captain Staple. I have been away from home a while, more than six years. I came back when I learned of my mother's death. That was almost six months ago. It took that long for me to get my brother's letter."

From the back of the room, Mike Wiley asked, "Are you Augustin Riff's daughter?"

Renata spun to face him. "You knew my father?"

"My father was a marine mechanic and did a few jobs for Mr. Riff. I'm Mike Wiley."

Renata settled back. "I know the name, but I don't know Staple. You must be new here, Captain."

"Compared to Mike," Ed said, and smiled. "Do you have other reasons for believing your life is in danger?"

Renata bowed her head. Ed let the silence stretch, waiting for her to go on when she was ready. For someone afraid for her life she seemed unusually cool. There was underlying emotion, however. Ed felt intrigued despite his sense of caution.

"My mother married Alban Revolo almost immediately after my father's death," Renata said, "although why she picked him . . ." The small blonde head tossed.

"That's not fair," Renata said, "Alban was nice enough for a gigolo. It's his son, Russell, who is the devil."

Ed looked at her in surprise. Revolo! Of course, with a name like that, it would have to be the same man.

"Is Russell Revolo your step-brother?" Ed asked.

"Yes. Do you know him?"

"Slightly. I bought an antique pine corner cupboard from him. It was purported to belong to his mother's family."

Renata shrugged. "Doubtless it did."

"You live in the old sea captain's house on Charter Street?"

"Yes."

"I remember the house. Very interesting place." He also remembered a very fine old Spanish chest that had stood in the entry foyer and wondered if the falling chandelier had damaged it.

"I suppose so," Renata said.

"I recall the chandelier you speak of, extremely heavy, hand wrought, at a guess, and beautifully done. There was also a carved Spanish chest. I trust it wasn't damaged."

Renata smiled. "A dent or two, nothing serious."

She looked at him, suddenly silent. The small head lifted in either pride or arrogance, and the fierceness came again into her eyes.

"My mother was Alva Rivera before she married. The Rivera family has been here from the beginning of the Mexican colonization. My father was of Spanish and English descent. He had been dead only a few months when my mother married Alban. Alban died a few months before Mother—or perhaps the way to say it is that she only survived him by a few months. At any rate, I came home to find Russell and his wife, Audrey, living in the house with my brother. Russell manages Adolf's finances. My brother is a diabetic."

"And your uncle also lives there?"

"Yes. Uncle Verian looks after the house-keeping and does the cooking. He was a professional chef by trade. It's a very cozy arrangement for all of them. Adolf has always been frail, and I'm afraid his illness has progressed alarmingly during the last few years. What time he doesn't spend in bed is devoted to writing a history of the early Mexican period in California."

Ed caught a note of irony in her words and thought, if she wasn't frightened, neither was she driven by anger. What was it about her? Let her talk, always the best way. If there was anything to this, it would come out. He was careful to keep his voice soft so as not to break her mood.

"Why do you believe one of these people wants to kill you, Miss Riff?"

Renata looking down at her weather rough-ened hands, put them self-consciously into the pockets of her jacket.

"I came home expecting to spend a couple of weeks and then move on. I would have, except for what happened last Sunday."

Renata glanced away from Ed, focusing on the scene visible through the office window.

The decision to come home had been made on impulse. She had not really been worried about Adolf, although she had thought it would be pleasant to see him again. They had been friends always.

She had stood on the sidewalk looking at the house, not thinking, not feeling, just standing there. The Riffs had been seamen and so the house was tall, three stories, with a captain's walk at the top. Inside, the ceilings were high and the staircases narrow and the rooms large and square.

Renata had let the memories of her room on the third floor come into her mind. She had loved her room, but that was all behind her. If she no longer belonged here, her going had been her own willful act, nevertheless, she decided she would go in. She would see it all once more. She had been glad of the decision, but on Sunday night her position as interloper had been painfully clear to her.

Ed repeated, "Miss Riff, why do you believe one of the people in your household wants to harm you?"

Renata's eyes blinked and focused on Ed.

"Because, after the chandelier fell, later that night, my brother came to my room, very upset, to warn me to leave."

"Then he too believes the chandelier was made to fall?"

"Either that, or he fears some similar accident will take place. But the falling chandelier is not what really brought me to you. Last Sunday night, Adolf confessed to me that I am my father's heir now that my mother is dead. I have since checked it out, and it is true. Everything went to my mother, but what I didn't know—or if I did, I had forgotten—was that it was a lifetime trust and at her death, because of Adolf's illness, everything comes to me. Out of the proceeds of the estate, I am to support Adolf and provide for his medical needs for his lifetime."

"You mean the attorney for the estate had not informed you of this?"

"No one except Adolf knew how to reach me, and all he had was a post office box number in San Francisco. I wrote to him once . . . maybe twice a year. It had been almost a year since he heard from me. I could have been dead. I feel sure he kept silent on instructions from Russell and Uncle Verian. I have, as I said, been away more than six years. In a few months it will be seven and I could have been declared legally dead."

The look of fierceness came back into her eyes and she kept her glance steadily on Ed.

"Captain Staple," Renata said, "I intend to stay and claim what is mine. In so doing, I may be putting my life in jeopardy. What I want you to know is that I am neither suicidal nor clumsy. I want you to believe that should I turn up dead some day, it will not be by suicide nor by accident, no matter how it is made to look. George Kettleman told me you have a thing against anyone getting away with murder. I want you to find my murderer—should he succeed."

2

Ed's right eyebrow lifted to a peak as he watched Mike and Renata leave his office together. While seeing her to her car, Mike would chat about Port Haven, old times and mutual friends, possibly picking up bits of information, but it was Ed's guess that Renata wouldn't give out with much.

"Well!" Ed thought, "She presents a challenge—if she's to be believed. Find her killer, if and when . . ."

Ed expelled a whistling sigh, an interesting household, certainly. She had given him a picture in which there were elements that might easily escalate into violence, but violence to whom by whom? Renata hardly seemed the typical passive victim. Did he believe her life was in jeopardy, or was she playing some game of her own? The signs of fear were less evident than the signs of aggressiveness. Or was that look of fierceness—that attitude of challenge—a cover-up? His general impression had been of a resolute defiance. Hummm. Resolute. That was a word. A little old-fashioned perhaps, nevertheless, he felt no need to search for another.

Revolo now. Russell, as he recalled, he had pigeonholed as a *dandy*—another old-fashioned word. Probably an association with the Riff house, the backdrop against which he had seen Russell, a darkly handsome man dressed with expensive, casual elegance. Ed conjured up Russell's face in his mind's eye and decided after a moment's thought that, at the time, he had been too preoccupied with the Riff house and the old pine cupboard to care about Russell the man. His recollection was that Russell was shrewd, perhaps cunning. Based on his memory, and today's interview, in a contest of wills between the two, Ed would be inclined to put his money on Renata.

"Quite a young lady," Ed said when Mike returned from escorting Renata downstairs to her car. "Do you know anything about her?"

"A little."

Mike pulled the chair Renata had occupied around so that he faced Ed at an oblique angle.

"There was a little flap about her after her father died, a baby maybe, or an abortion.

Then she disappeared, so far as I know."

"Remember who the fellow was?"

"Nope. Wouldn't swear there was one. It's just sort of an impression more than a memory. Her father I do recall. He had a commercial fishing boat. My father knew him well and liked him, a big, rough man, but kind in lots of ways, and honest. I knew Mrs. Riff by sight. A beautiful, voluptuous type, very sexy—or so I thought as a kid."

"Did you know her second husband?"

Mike extended a hand and rocked it back and forth. "Yes and no. He came to town as a dance instructor—one of those chain operations. One of his most successful projects was a jazz dance class for the young matrons in town. My guess is that's where they met."

That explained the remark about the gigolo, Ed thought. He said, "Renata obviously didn't approve the match."

"Seems I recall my dad saying something about Augustin Riff's daughter. They must have been pretty close. He took her fishing summers, I think."

"What about the brother?"

Mike shrugged. "Older by three or four years, and like she said, a diabetic. Stayed pretty close to mamma, I guess. I can't recall my dad mentioning him being about the boat."

"How about the others?"

"Russell Revolo and old Verian? I know Verian like I know Dad Schooner. They both play the horses and frequent Lile's Pool Parlor. They're both around. The Riveras and the Riffs have always been here. You grew up knowing about them, but there has been enough money to put them outside the everyday folk. And there is the heritage bit. The Riveras were Castillian Spanish and have pretty well kept the line clean, at least the male line. Alva, Renata's mother, was one of a flock of girls, so I guess she got to marry anyone she wanted. The head of the family lives in Santa Barbara and I guess the rest are scattered."

Mike studied the toe of his lightly polished brogues. "Russell I don't know. He went to college somewhere and he works for an accounting firm in Santa Barbara. His wife is some kind of therapist in Ventura. Works for the county, I think."

There was evidently enough truth in Renata's story to merit a look-see. "You'd better check them all out," Ed said, "and I'll talk with George Kettleman, maybe take him to lunch."

Ed reached for the phone, and Mike pushed his lean, hard-muscled body from his chair, stretching to his full five feet eleven. As he passed the office door, Mike paused a few seconds to look at his reflection in the glass upper half. He straightened his tie and smoothed one of his crisp waves of brown hair back into place, then he moved on.

Renata Riff watched Mike Wiley until the back door of the County Building closed behind him. She was driving the Mercedes that had belonged to her mother. Alva had loved prestige cars. Her father had always driven a pickup. Renata started the car and drove out of the parking lot. Without any conscious intent, she wound through the streets, crossing the railroad tracks to Marlin Street to come out on the waterfront near the wharf. She found a parking place along the curb, but didn't get out of the car for a long time.

It had changed little. The Marsden Cannery Building with its cranes and sheds dominated the lower wharf side of the street with a row of small businesses strung out toward her and the railroad spur cutting through on an angle. There were fishing boats tied up along both fingers of pier. The *Spring Tide* and the *Dolly McBain* she knew. Only a few people moved about at mid-morning. It was still coffee break time and those who could would be at the cafe across the street swapping stories and gossip.

Renata rolled down the car window to let the smells and sounds of this once familiar place drift in on the moist air. The cannery was silent. Operations had been limited to processing sports fishermen's catches for many years and may have shut down entirely during her absence, although the fishing fleet obviously still operated. She could hear the gentle slap of water against the piles of the wharf and the short fingers of pier. Marsden had always kept the wharf clean. There was no smell of putrified fish, only the clean iodine scent of salt water and the mustiness of old wet wood came through the open window.

Renata opened the door and got out to walk along the wharf to the pier where *The Alva*'s berth had been. Her mother had sold the boat almost immediately. A wise move actually, but one that had hurt Renata.

At her approach a sea gull launched itself from the piling at the end of the dock, crying in protest as it circled and came down again on the edge of the wharf fifty feet away. Renata examined the top of the piling where the gull had roosted, saw that it was clean, and leaned her elbows on it. She looked out to sea, but her thoughts were anchored in the past: her father, too big and strong to think he would ever die; the summers he took her on board *The Alva* as deck hand; the hard work and the laughter. It had been so good.

"Renata!"

The voice cut into her reverie, spinning her around to face a young man with curling brown hair and mild blue eyes who stood smiling at her. He had a short nose and a short upper lip, which gave his face a slightly pug look. His shoulders were broad under his flannel shirt. The faded blue jeans he wore fit snugly around the slender hips and good straight legs, spread a little apart, as if he balanced himself on a rolling deck.

"Hey," he said, and holding up a hand, palm up, he took a step backward. "Hey," he repeated. "I just thought I'd say 'hello'."

It took a moment for recognition to come, before the fear drained away and she relaxed.

"Bart Cameron," Renata said, and smiled.

She stood still, looking at him, drinking him in like a glass of good cold water after hours in the sun. Bart Cameron. She hadn't allowed herself to think of him in years. And since she had come home, there had been too many other things.

Bart said, "I thought for a minute you were going to attack me. Is something the matter, Renata?"

Slowly, she shook her head. "No, I was just so lost in memories, you startled me. I had no idea you'd still be here. Tell me about yourself. Do you have time? Could I buy you a cup of coffee while we catch up?"

When they were seated across from each other in a booth in a waterfront cafe, Renata reached out a hand and Bart took it in his. He turned her hand over, smoothing the calloused palm with his finger tips.

"Now tell me everything," Renata said, then paused and withdrew her hand from his. "You aren't married, are you?" she asked.

"No. Are you?"

She shook her head. "Are you still fishing?"

"I go out when I can. I'm still going to own a boat some day."

She smiled and settled back in the booth without touching the coffee.

"College?" she asked.

He nodded, and she thought, *I missed all that. I've missed so much.*

Bart said, "I took your father's advice and learned the carpenter trade from my father. I put myself through college that way. I'm between jobs now, but I like the building business and I think I'll go after my contractor's license. I don't like being in an office all day, although I took my degree in Business Administration and Accounting."

"How is your family?"

"Everybody's fine. I'm the only one at home, the other six have scattered, although most of them live nearby."

She couldn't take her eyes off him. The smile felt fixed on her face, but she seemed unable to change it. To be sitting here opposite Bart in an ordinary way was a fantasy. It couldn't be real. She reached out her hand again and he took it, smiling at her, the look in his eyes gentle as always.

"Now, what's with you? Where have you been all these years? What happened? You just disappeared."

"I know. Maybe some day I'll tell you about it. Maybe, if I'm lucky. Anyway, I'm home for a while, until I can get Dad's estate settled, then I'll have to see."

She squeezed his hand. "Bart, it's good to see you."

He grinned, then laughed. "I wasn't so sure there for a few minutes when I first spoke to you."

He stopped speaking for a few moments while he studied her intently.

"There had to be something more than surprise that made you turn like that. You're afraid of someone, aren't you?"

"Let it go, Bart. Don't ask questions, okay?"

His smile was tentative, then broadened. "Okay, if you'll have dinner with me."

Renata relaxed and laughed. "We were going to do that six years ago, remember?"

"Yeah, I remember."

They stared at each other in silence.

"Well?" Bart said.

"All right."

"I'll pick you up at six."

"Oh Bart . . . Oh, this must be that place somewhere over the rainbow."

Only then did Renata realize they were still holding hands.

Renata took her purchases upstairs to show them to Adolf. The dress was a simple shirtwaist of boucle knit in a pretty delft blue. She had bought shoes and a small blue handbag.

"I forgot a jacket," Renata said. "Do you think the dress will be warm enough?"

"Sure. You'll be in a car or an air-conditioned building. Unless Bart's taking you to Der Wienerschnitzle," Adolf said, and laughed.

Renata laughed with her brother and said,

"No chance. This is going to be a real date."

"Bart Cameron," Adolf said. "I haven't thought of him in years. He's a carpenter, did you say?"

"A carpenter with a degree in Business Administration and Accounting. Anyway, I'm sure he can afford it now."

Renata picked up her packages to take them to her room.

"I had a string of pearls once," she said. "I wonder if they are in with Mother's jewelry."

"Why don't you have a look?"

"Will you go with me?"

Adolf smiled as he got up from his desk. "Sure, come on."

When Alva's jewelry box had been found and placed on her dressing table, Renata said, "Will you open it, please Adolf? I feel as if I'm trespassing." And then when it was open she said, "I'd no idea there was so much. These things shouldn't have been left in the house."

Adolf held up two strings of pearls. "Either of these yours?"

"Yes. The little baby ones. Seed pearls, Dad called them."

"Oh, yes, I remember. For your sixteenth birthday, weren't they."

"Yes. His last gift to me."

Adolf dropped them into her outstretched hand.

"They're interesting, but they're small and sort of irregular. Sure you wouldn't rather wear the perfect ones?"

"Mother's? No."

"They're yours now. It's all yours."

"Ours," Renata said. "I'm just the administrator of the estate."

Adolf dropped the pearls back into the case, put a hand over his heart and sat down on the dressing table bench.

"What's the matter?" Renata demanded. "Did you take your insulin? Did you eat lunch?"

"Yes. Yes to both questions. I've been very careful about everything. It's my heart. Close up that box and help me get to my room, will you? I'll be all right if I lie down for a while."

While she closed up the jewelry box and put it away, Renata said, "I'm getting you to a specialist. I know Dr. Craig is okay, but I'll feel better with a second opinion, and I don't think he'll mind."

Later, when Renata went downstairs to tell Verian she wouldn't be home for dinner, she spoke to him about Adolf's heart.

"Flutters a bit now and then," Verian said. "Nothing to be overly alarmed about. We all keep a pretty close watch on the boy, and Craig's here once a week regular."

"He just seems so much worse than I remembered."

"Well he is, Renata. He probably won't live to be forty."

Verian was preparing veal for dinner, scallopini for himself and the Revolos and a special portion for Adolf, saltless and sauce-less, but with vegetables and a salad, all attractively arranged and as palatable as possible. Verian went to great pains in preparing Adolf's evening meal.

While he worked in the kitchen, Verian wore his chef's hat and a white jacket. He wasn't as tall as Renata's father had been, nor was he as broad of shoulder, but he had the sandy hair and the good looks of the Riff men. Renata had liked her uncle since he first came to live with them more than ten years ago.

"I think he should see a specialist."

Verian took the saute pan from the stove and turned to face her.

"Look Renata, I understood your feeling for your father, and God knows what happened to you shouldn't happen to the worst heathen on earth, but you made a choice. You could have stayed at home, even if you wouldn't do what your mother wanted, or you could have gone away to college like you were supposed to. Now don't come back here and expect everyone to fall all over themselves to welcome you. We liked it the way we had it. It was a good deal for us all. There's nothing anybody can do for Adolf more than take care of him for as long as he lives. A specialist would put him through a lot of unpleasant tests that wouldn't help him in the long run and would wear him down more. Why don't you just back off, at least for a while? Okay?"

Verian returned to his cooking, and after a

moment while she stared at his back, Renata left the kitchen. She was already dressed and it was still a quarter to six. She would have to wait in the living room or climb the stairs again to her bedroom on the third floor. While she waited, Russell came into the room.

"Hello, Renata. My! The heiress has been shopping. Very nice. *Very* nice."

He walked over to the small bar that had been installed during her absence, and began to mix himself a drink.

"Will you join me?"

"No thanks, I'm going out."

"Oh? Really? Anyone I know?"

"I doubt it. And for the record, I spent my own money. The estate hasn't been turned over to me yet."

"True, but meanwhile, you can doubtless have sufficient funds released to you for reasonable expenditures."

"I may do that. Thanks for the suggestion."

"No need to be huffy," Russell said.

He took his drink to his favorite chair and sat down.

"I suppose you're naturally upset with all of us, not telling you about the will. It was foolish. The attorney would have found you eventually. However, neither Verian nor I knew about Adolf's correspondence with you until after the attorney began to ask questions, and that was only a couple of months ago. Naturally, since it had been over six months, and you hadn't answered Adolf's

letter, we . . ." He sipped his drink and smiled at her. "We persuaded Adolf to leave it up to the attorney and hoped for the best—from our point of view, that is."

"And when I showed up, you persuaded Adolf to wait, hoping I would go away."

"It was reasonable to assume that you would. You even said so when you first came."

Had she? Perhaps. It didn't matter because the Revolos wouldn't be staying long. There were legal matters that had to come first. Then she would tell Russell.

"I do hope you can let by-gones be by-gones and we can all get along peaceably."

If only he didn't look so much like his father, Renata thought. He even sounded like Alban Revolo. Seeing him, hearing him, brought it all back. Her mother, Alban, her father dead less than three months. She would never be able to tolerate this. She would always see his father in him.

"I don't think you should look on this as a permanent arrangement, Russell," Renata said, and knew immediately that she had made a cardinal mistake. Whatever her feelings or her plans for the future, Russell should be the last to know.

3

George Kettleman had been unavailable for lunch, so Ed Staple arranged to meet him for dinner at the Downtowner Hotel restaurant. Then, Ed decided to see what John Silas, the Riff's attorney, had to say. John, who was five-seven, sixtyish, with a cockscomb of crisply waving gray hair, was affectionately known as the *Bantom Rooster*. Once in John's office, Ed wasted no time in preliminaries, he told John in crisp, succinct language of his interview with Renata. Then he listened while John said a great deal about withheld information and his ability to get a conviction, if allowed.

"Renata won't prosecute because of her brother, but they should be hauled into court, the lot of them. Six months, Ed—six months I busted my butt trying to find that girl, and all the time Adolf sat there with that San Francisco Post Office box number. I hired detectives, checked the missing persons bureaus all over the country, had APB's put out. Had the CHP alerted. I turned every stone, and there he sat with that P.O. box number all the time. Ought to be jailed, diabetic or no."

"Do you think your client is in any danger from her family, John?"

The bantam rooster quieted. "Well Ed, the desire may be there. That is, they may all wish she had turned up dead, or not turned up at all, but I can't say I really believe the chandelier was made to fall. Neither Russell nor Verian has what it takes to pull off a thing like that. I'd say it depends on how generous the new heiress is. She should throw out the lot, but if she isn't going to, then she'd better be prepared to be generous."

"Do you know where she's been for over six years?"

"Nope."

"For the last six months?"

"Yup. Been working on a fishing boat off the coast of South America."

"A woman . . ." Ed began.

"Her daddy taught her the trade. She probably pulled her fair share of the freight, but I know what you mean. Ship's captain had been a friend of her father's. She said she needed a safe place."

"A place safe from what?"

John spread his hands in a gesture of resignation.

"She told me what I've told you, then she told me if I needed to know more, she'd tell me when I needed to know it. She told me just about like that."

Ed grinned. John laughed, and Ed joined in.

"I knew her father, of course, so I didn't argue too much. I want to retain my position as her counsel."

A vision of Renata and John together floated into Ed's mind, a bantam rooster and hen going at each other. He laughed. "Why did she leave home?" he asked.

"She took Augustin's death very hard. They were—maybe too close. When her mother married Alban Revolo so soon, Renata just couldn't take it. Went kind of wild . . ."

John stopped, looked away from Ed a moment, then back.

"Renata had a very unfortunate experience which may account for her disappearance without a trace, but the basic cause was Alva's remarriage."

"What happened to her?" Ed asked.

John shook his head. "Water under the bridge, Ed. Nothing to do with today. To quote my fiery young client, I'll tell you if you ever need to know. Until then, I think the best way to keep my client is to keep my mouth shut."

Very soon afterward, Ed thanked John and left the attorney's office.

The rough hands and the sun bleached hair were explained. Ed tried to picture Renata as a deck hand on board a fishing boat and found he could do it. The trim, firm body vibrated with life despite its diminutive size. She was, he thought, both strong and athletic. He could also picture her coming off the boat, her duffel bag over her shoulder, making for the post office. He could imagine her taking the letter from the box. He could imagine her reading it; see quick tears form, to be wiped away on the non-absorbent nylon jacket sleeve. Sorrow and longings came with the loss of even an estranged mother. He could understand the sudden desire to go home, to touch base once more.

He was getting too involved with this small, fiery enigma named Renata. He was not entirely sure she could be trusted. He couldn't entirely put aside the possibility that she was using him and his office.

Ed arrived first at the Downtowner Hotel restaurant, and chose a booth where he and George Kettleman would have some privacy. When the bourbon and water he ordered came but George did not, Ed let his thoughts wander over what he had already begun to think of as "The Riff Case."

If you were a cop long enough, Ed thought, you developed a "feel" about a case. It came with the job, with seeing so many people in so many high stress situations. Experience taught you what the likely responses would be. It was probably the same in many professions. Doctors looked at you and knew if you had high blood pressure, or were running a fever. Mechanics listened to you car's motor and knew what was wrong. This case was a wrong one. Ed had his guard up, no getting away from it. While he waited for George, he wondered why.

What he felt wasn't a hunch, it wasn't that definite. What was eating him, if he wanted to admit it, was his lack of sympathy. A diminutive creature like that bravely fighting for her life. At the least he should feel admiration for her wit and spirit. Oh well, if he didn't feel it, he thought it; besides, most probably nothing would come of all this.

On the surface, it looked simple enough. Renata's homecoming had thrown a monkey wrench into a pretty well oiled machine. He agreed with John Silas that the old chandelier had fallen of its own weight, and believed Renata felt as they did—it was a freak accident, nothing more. What it had accomplished was, it had set Adolf thinking.

If the falling chandelier had brought on Adolf's confession, then it must be presumed that there was real danger to Renata in the situation, either expressed or implied, or why did Adolf feel as he did? What Ed should be worrying about was how to prevent a possible homicide, certainly there was money enough for motive, and proximity gave opportunity. Maybe the picture would clear up after he talked with George.

George Kettleman came in and was directed to Ed's booth. Ed stood and they shook hands.

"Been waiting long?" George asked.

"A few minutes. Gave me time to think."

They were about the same height, although Ed was heavier, and in spite of their difference in facial type and coloring, each had the same look of controlled vitality. George's exuberant red curls had been expertly styled to behave. His smooth good looks and light blue eyes invited confidence. The two men smiled at each other and sat down.

They talked of generalities during cocktails, then when the entree was served, Ed told George that Renata Riff had come to visit him.

"From what she said, I gather she talked with you first. Are you convinced her life is in danger?"

George cleared his throat. "Are you asking off the cuff, or in your official capacity?"

"I won't know until I get the answers to a few questions."

"I see. Well, the Riff family has banked with us for a number of years. After Mrs. Revolo's death the bank was appointed interim trustee for the Riff estate pending notification of the principal heir, Adolf Riff being a virtual invalid, so I am somewhat familiar with the situation."

"If you are the trustee for the estate, how does Russell Revolo come in as managing Adolf's financial affairs?"

"Mrs. Revolo had a small estate of her own which went directly to her son."

"Had she disinherited her daughter?"

"I doubt that there was anything formal, although there was a definite break between the two."

"Do you know what caused it?"

"The marriage to Revolo was the initial break, I think."

"And after that?"

"We're neighbors, Captain, but that doesn't mean I knew what was going on in the Riff household. I knew them all by sight, and Augustin and Alva as substantial depositors in the bank. I liked Augustin and was surprised when his wife remarried so soon. I was also surprised at her choice. I only became aware that Renata had left home for good some time after she had returned the first time."

"How did this come to your attention?"

"Mrs. Revolo told me."

"Where had Renata been?"

"She didn't say."

"Was this a friendly back fence conversation?"

"No. Mrs. Revolo had come into the bank to make certain financial arrangements for Renata."

"George, you're making me pull this out bit by bit."

George smiled and repeated his question. "Is this a friendly chat, or an official investigation?"

"There has been no complaint filed, if that's what you want to know."

"Then, old friend, I think I have gone as far as I can without some better reason than that you asked. At the time, Mrs. Revolo asked that the arrangements made with the bank be kept confidential, and so as trustee for the estate, I feel obliged to follow these instructions."

"How long are you required to keep records on file?"

"Five years."

I'd like to see those records, Ed thought, feeling convinced Alva's financial arrangements would tell him a great deal. Maybe he could get at it another way.

"Since it was a back fence conversation with you that sent Renata to us, mind telling me about it?"

"Glad to."

Ed waited. George waited.

"In your own words," Ed said.

"Beginning . . . ?"

"At the beginning, if you will, please."

"Have this cat," George said, "big blue Maltese tom. I was looking for him to take him to have his nails trimmed. Naturally he hid. Renata was outside, coaxed him to her (unheard of before) and handed him to me over the fence. Next time I saw her outside, I thanked her, naturally we chatted a bit. That was on Sunday afternoon. On Monday just before closing time, her attorney, John Silas, came in to inform us that the missing Riff heir had returned. Later at home, I was outside looking for Sir Thomas again . . ."

"Sir Thomas is the cat?"

"Knights of Malta, you know. Tom cat. Sir Thomas."

"Logical," Ed said, and smiled. "He was with Renata again, was he?"

"Thomas has taken quite a shine to Renata. She seems to be outside a lot. Anyway, I expressed my pleasure that she had returned, explaining who I was and what the bank's duties had been."

"She didn't know who you were before?"

George shook his head. "I had said, 'I'm George,' and introduced Sir Thomas, and said I hoped he hadn't been a nuisance. She had said, 'I'm Renata,' that she liked cats and he was quite a specimen."

"Okay," Ed said, "when you got around to complete identification, did she say where she'd been?"

"She said if I was glad of her return I was the only one. I was polite and reassuring, and she laughed and told me about the chandelier falling."

"What do you make of that?"

"Accident most likely, considering the inmates of that house."

"Then why did you send her to me?"

"Well, I asked her how her family was taking things. In the conversation she mentioned how she learned she was her father's heir. What she said was they hadn't given her the glad tidings immediately upon her arrival. I made appropriate leading comments and she confessed she intended sleeping lightly, watching her footing on the stairs, and eating only out of the common dish. In short, she expects foul play. That's when I suggested you. In addition, I had another reason."

Ed looked at George without comment. He was wondering what would have happened had he asked in the beginning, "Why?" There was a lesson somewhere in all this he was going to have to think about. For now, he would play George's straight man.

"What other reason?" Ed asked.

"When I remodeled my old house some years ago, I put in a pool. I was lounging around on a Sunday afternoon last August, I think it was, when I heard two people in the Riff back yard. They were talking. I couldn't hear it all, but it was a man and a woman. They seemed to be strolling, and as they passed near be I could hear distinctly."

The waiter removed their plates, and George ordered coffee and brandy. When they were alone again, Ed asked, "What did you overhear, George?"

"The woman was talking as they approached, but I didn't get the beginning. She said, ' . . . withholding information and isn't that a crime?' The man said, 'Who's going to prosecute?' The woman said, 'They're sure to find her.' The man said, 'Maybe not if Tanner . . .' I'm not positive about the accuracy of my recollection here, but I think he said,

. . . finds her first.' By that time they were moving out of earshot again."

Ed said, "Was the couple the Revolos, Russell and Audrey?"

"Didn't see them, couldn't swear to it," George said, "but talking with Renata, I recalled what I had overheard, and that's why I thought I'd better suggest that she see you."

"Who is Tanner?" Ed asked.

George shrugged. "No idea."

The waiter brought coffee and brandies, and when he moved aside, Ed was startled to see Renata—a different, groomed and personable Renata—and a young man being seated the third booth up from them.

George said, "What's happening?"

Ed held up a restraining hand. "Easy. Renata came in with a young man. Take your time and see who he is, he's facing us."

After a moment, George looked around. "Bart Cameron," he said. "Nice young man. Worked his way through college helping his dad carpenter—we made him a loan to help out. Going for his contractor's license, he told me. Does some commercial fishing. Probably knew Renata before. Probably went to school together."

There was one consistent feature of the Riff case, Ed thought. It was full of surprises.

It was close to midnight when Renata let herself into the old Riff house using the keys that had been her father's. She didn't immediately climb the stairs, but went into the living room. She reached the front window in time to see the tail lights of Bart's car flash on as he braked for the corner, then they disappeared as he made the turn.

Along about dessert, Renata had realized that Bart was going to want to kiss her goodnight. They had told her that one day, when it was the right young man, she would enjoy being kissed. If there was ever going to be a right young man, it was Bart. By the time they had finished their coffee, she had made up her mind to give it a try, although the thought of it made her sweat.

They had been right. Kissing Bart was sensational. Kissing Bart gave her a glowing feeling. So, after six years she had had a normal reaction to a man—to Bart.

"Slow, Renata," she told herself, "take it a step at a time. Don't panic. Don't panic."

Renata turned from the window and left the living room. She climbed the stairs to the second floor and had started up to the third when Adolf's voice said, "Renata?"

She didn't reply, but went to the door of his room. Adolf was in bed, propped up with pillows. He didn't look well. She crossed over to him quickly.

"Dolf, are you all right?"

He nodded. "Yes, I'm all right, but I wanted to talk to you."

"Now? It's almost midnight."

"Yes. Now."

She sat on the side of his bed. "You don't

have to tell me," she said. "It's Russell."

"He says you plan to force him to go away."

Renata gave a little laugh. "He would put it like that."

"Are you?"

"He reminds me of his father," Renata said.

"I don't want him to go, Renata. He's been a very good friend to me. I depend on him. I don't want you to send him away."

Renata reached out and touched her brother's hand. "Adolf . . ."

He withdrew his hand.

"I wish I hadn't told you about the inheritance. Russell was right, you're going to try to mess up everything. Well, I'm not going to let you, Renata. I'm not going to let you send Russell away."

Renata sat very still on the side of her brother's bed. He looked so ill, she could hardly believe he had deteriorated so much in six years. With all the wonders of modern medicine you would think Adolf would be getting better. She was going to call in a specialist. She didn't care what Verian said.

"Don't get so worked up, Dolf," Renata said. "I'm not going to throw your precious Russell out into the street. But remember, it was because of his influence that you didn't tell John Silas about my post office box in San Francisco. I find that hard to forget."

Adolf looked down at the sheets, pinching them with his long white hands.

"We were very happy here together until you came," he said. "Please, Renata, don't mess things up for me. Please."

4

At nine forty-five on Thursday morning of the second week in November, Det. Sergeant Mike Wiley knocked before he entered Ed Staple's office, although the door was open as usual.

"Captain, you got a minute?" Mike asked, and noticed that today Ed's vest was that shade of taupe that looked smart with navy blue. The captain was having one of his thoughtful days.

"All the time in the world," Ed said.

"About Russell Revolo," Mike said, as he put a small sheaf of papers on Ed's desk. "There doesn't seem to be much of anything there. Russell banks for Adolf, writes his checks to pay household expenses. There's a five figure bank account and a nice income on which Russell signs as executor. The bank account looks okay. Verian Riff has a generous allowance, but the word is, he owes money. I haven't found out how much, or to whom, but what I hear is Verian was unlucky at the race track a couple of times. Guesses vary as to the amount from two to twenty thou. Word is, it's not the first time, and before, Russell bailed him out with Adolf's money. If he did, it doesn't show on the bank statements, so it must have been run through as a legitimate expense. You want me to go any further? We have no complaint on file."

Ed sat down and riffled through the sheaf of papers. Mike's written report was stapled to sheets with vital statistics for Russell and Audrey Revolo and Adolf, Renata and Verian Riff.

Ed said, "Renata came into the Downtowner Hotel restaurant Tuesday night with a young man. Bart Cameron, according to George Kettleman. Know him?"

"Know who he is," Mike said and sat down.

They discussed the Riff case for the next fifteen minutes, then Ed said, "No need to go any further for now, but put out the word that we'd be interested in anything unusual, especially if anyone calls in Verian's debt.

"Yes, sir," Mike said.

Ed leaned back in his chair.

"I've been thinking of taking tomorrow off for a hunting trip up on Padre Mountain."

"A good time for it, Captain. Things are sure quiet. Makes you think about he lull before the storm, and the Thanksgiving holidays will be coming up soon."

Ed watched Mike leave the office. His detective-sergeant was a capable officer, too good for a small town, but there was no way Mike was going to leave Port Haven. He'd been born in the town, loved it, and wanted to raise his own family here.

The calendar on Ed's desk was the perpetual kind. You turned one wheel for the day and date, another for the month, and another for the year. Ed pulled the calendar to him, made the necessary changes and sat staring unseeing, wondering what there was about the date he should remember. After a few seconds, it came to him.

"Five years!" he said aloud, and chuckled as he pushed the calendar back into its accustomed spot on the desk. Five years on a temporary job. Ed had thought of it that way at the time, as something he needed, like getting back on a horse that has thrown you.

On the far edge of the desk, facing the door, there was a bronze nameplate that read: Captain Edward G. Staple. Five years ago there had been no nameplate at all. They (his men) had given this one to him on his first anniversary.

Five years. Well, maybe not to the day, but on the first Thursday in November he had walked into this office for the first time, an outsider, twenty-two months removed from his former employment with the San Diego Police Department, hired to do a job.

At that time, the bullet wounds in his back

that had almost ended his life had healed, but the hurt from the divorce was still a steady ache and the questions the two events had raised in his mind about both himself and his job had nagged him. He supposed they always would, still he had been glad to be back at work.

There had been an excitement about those first months. Two teenagers dead, OD'd on heroin, and somebody local had to be responsible. He could have completed his job within a dozen days, but small communities were always suspect of outsiders. It had taken three months of tactful politicking and a little firm, quiet pressure in the right places before he had his proof and his indictment. Even then, it would have been next to impossible without help from, then "Deputy" Mike Wiley. With Mike's help, he had cleaned up the station and the town. And, he had kept it clean. Clean and quiet. Maybe too quiet.

Ed riffled through the stack of reports on his desk, then went to the west window that gave him a view of the north point of Refugio Bay and the arc around the yacht basin breakwater. November sunshine was soft and mild through the overcast. The sea was calm—as calm as the town.

Ed watched a sailboat change tack. It was a lovely view. Port Haven was a nice town. He liked it. He liked the camaraderie he had with the men of the community, a rare commodity for a peace officer today. Nevertheless, Ed was bored . . .

Maybe it was time for him to move on. Perhaps he should go back to a city job, some place where the action was.

Or maybe the root of his boredom and restlessness was fear that he was falling in love again. After Marie Elena . . . well . . . Ed rammed his hands into his pockets, his big body gone rigid as he stared out the window. He never wanted to see that kind of hurt and misery in another woman's eyes, not because he was a cop.

Ed turned from the window and began to go through the report Mike had left on his desk. It was time for a hunting trip. Or was that an excuse to get him up on Padre Mountain where it would be easy and logical to stop by the Cold Creek Trout Farm for a visit with Jamie Hartfield?

Ed pushed Mike's report away from him, disgusted with himself. What kind of machinations was he going through? If he wanted to see the girl, why not go?

At six-ten on that Thursday evening, Verian Riff left the kitchen and went into the living room where Russell was mixing a drink for himself. Verian stood where he could see into the entry in case Renata should come downstairs.

"I need some cash, Russell," Verian said. "I lost a bundle that last time I went to the races, and the boys want their money."

Russell's lips smiled as he spoke, but his eyes held a stony look.

"You picked a hell of a time," he said.

"How'd I know she was going to show up?"

Russell moved his hand in a slicing motion.

"I warned you, Verian," he said, "there's just so much I can do with Adolf's account. You'll have to practice a little patience."

"Yeah," Verian said. "I will—now."

Russell drank from the glass he held. Verian looked through the door into the entry.

"Well, how about it?" Verian said. "I need five thousand in cash."

Russell said, "Five thousand!"

He crossed the room to stand in front of Verian, eyes blazing with anger.

"My God, man, what do you think I am, a magician?"

Verian didn't move, didn't flicker an eyelid.

"Something like that," he said.

Russell said, "I don't think I can do it. Renata has been talking to the sheriff, and Mike Wiley has been nosing around the bank. When must you have the money?"

"Next week."

"No way," Russell said. "Can you stall?"

"I've been stalling."

Russell drank and paced.

"You may have to go direct to Adolf," he said. "When was the last time you made a touch?"

Verian shrugged. "Before his mother died. Nothing big."

Russell sighed. "Stall as long as you can,

then do it. Be ashamed and sorry and afraid of Renata, okay?"

Verian grinned. "Okay."

"And for heaven's sake, man, stick to the penny ante stuff until things settle down."

Verian nodded, and returned to the kitchen.

On Friday, after work, Ed stopped to buy shells and spent a relaxed and congenial half hour at First's Gun Shop talking guns and deer, arriving home in time for a swim before Suzanna, his cook and housekeeper, put dinner on the table.

After only twenty laps, Ed quit, toweled off, and entered his house through the French doors opening into the hallway off his bedroom. The pine cupboard stood in a corner of this small area. Ed paused to look at it fondly. Handcrafted and severely plain, it was just right for the space and for the overflow of his collection of duck decoys.

One of the decoys was a canvasback with a "pistol-grip" head. Although crudely carved, it was one of his favorites. Ed picked it up, running his fingers over the wood of the body. He replaced it, rubbed his hand over the soft pine of the cupboard, and thought of Russell Revolo.

During the past three days he had tried repeatedly to form a clearer opinion of the man, but nothing had come to him. The old

Riff house was what had held his attention, what he'd seen of it.

Soon after Ed bought the house on Chapala Street, Suzanna had moved into the apartment over the garage and taken over the running of his household. She was an adequate housekeeper and excellent cook. Suzanna's cooking kept him home nights.

Friday nights Suzanna cooked American. There was always a roast of sufficient proportions to give Ed meat through the weekend should he want it. Tonight there were uncut green beans cooked until tender, together with the dutchess potatoes and the tomato and green onion garnish, the effect was totally appetizing. Ed sighed with deep contentment and smiled up at Suzanna as she poured burgundy into the wine goblet at his plate.

"You staying home again this weekend?" Suzanna asked.

"I'm going hunting."

"You got a girl?"

"I've always got a girl."

Suzanna closed her eyes and shook her head. "A woman, yes. You've been home every weekend for a month. You've got a girl. Are you going to get married?"

"What would I want with a wife when I've got you?"

"For your bedroom," Suzanna smiled benignly and returned to the kitchen.

Ed ate his meal with less enjoyment than he might have, then retreated to his living room for his brandy and cigar. The Riff case troubled him. Renata's missing six, almost seven years were tantalizing questions. Evidently both Silas and Kettleman knew more than they were willing to tell. Oh, well, give it time.

Ed picked up the book he was currently reading, but tonight it failed to hold his interest. To keep his mind off the Riff case, he went to the garage and packed the jeep for his trip up the mountain. These short jaunts suited him, getting him out of doors without having to join a hunting party and travel great distances.

It was on just such a hunting trip that he had found Jamie. He had first seen her with the slanting rays of the early morning sun making a halo of light around her pale yellow hair. Her eyes, set wide apart, were the blue of summer skies. Her mouth was also wide, the soft pink lips slightly parted. Five-seven in height, his eyes measured, with an angular figure, slender, but not thin. She wore a faded blue sweatshirt and blue jeans, the legs stuffed into short rain boots. Recalling Jamie's rough clothing reminded Ed of Renata. For a few moments he compared the two women and felt amused that he could see similarities. They were both independent spirits.

Ed dropped Renata from his thoughts. Jamie was indelibly printed in his memory, a mythological creature standing at the edge of a small clearing, warning him that he trespassed on private property. They had talked only briefly before she asked him to have breakfast with her. Before going inside, she had shown him the trout farm that was her inheritance from an uncle. The house was a 1930 bungalow built of stone, small but comfortable. The first thing Ed saw when he went inside was a cabinet filled to overflowing with duck decoys. Decoys were sitting everywhere.

"Uncle collected them," Jamie said.

Ed had held his breath and asked, "Would you be interested in selling them?"

Jamie had given him a pitying look and shook her head. "Oh, dear. You're a collector. Poor man."

For answer, Ed had said, "I can't believe this." He stooped down to examine a decoy resting on the floor beside the cabinet.

"Do you realize what this is?"

"Oh yes, it's Indian, probably from the Chesapeake Bay area, made from reeds, and is likely a thousand years old."

He looked up at her, knowing he was pleading. She had laughed, not unkindly, and said, "Sorry, I'm not interested in selling anything."

He had slowly given up his hope of buying the decoys, but he had continued to visit the stone house on the mountain.

Ed had known her six months before he made love to her. With Jamie there was no overwhelming ecstasy of passion, but a mutual consent born of time spent together.

To touch her body sent no wild desire through him, only a quiet pleasure. There was nothing erotic in their love play, yet invariably she left him replete, filled with contentment and peace. Since she stirred in his body no hot, demanding desire, he wondered, did the need to be near her come from the soul? If that were true, it was doubly frightening.

Ed finished packing the jeep and left the garage. The pool shimmered darkly under a half moon. He stripped quickly and plunged in, swam a dozen laps, emerged dripping, gathered up his clothes and ran, shivering into the house.

Before noon on Sunday, Ed thought as he grew warm under the covers of his bed, after he got his deer he would drive the jeep over the track up the ridge, come out on the fire-break and drop down to the Cold Creek Trout Farm. By dinnertime Sunday he would have spun out all his frustrations, including the Riff case, and after doing the dishes, he and Jamie would sit in companionable silence before the fire with her uncle's incredible duck decoys their equally silent companions. They would sit on the love seat, bodies touching. At some point in time, his arm would go around her, pulling her close. They would kiss, and that would be the beginning.

Ed turned beneath the covers, sleep only seconds away. When sleep came, it brought not dreams of Jamie, but of Renata. He saw her first, Cheshire cat style, that fierce, proud light in her eyes, her smile flashing on and off. The head faded to be replaced by kaleidoscopic pictures of Renata as she appeared in his office, as she jumped from beneath the falling chandelier, as she walked into the restaurant, and then on board a fishing boat. She was grinning broadly as she hauled in a line on which a fish floundered. When she pulled it over the ship's railing, it had a fish's body but his own face. Ed came totally awake, his whole body sweating.

5

Bart Cameron asked Renata to go fishing on the first Wednesday of December.

"Marvelous," she said. "We'll make a day of it."

Verian obligingly packed a feast suitable for eating on board a Boston whaler and had it in the basket for Renata at seven in the morning.

"I'm taking the day off myself," he told her.

She paused and looked at him in dismay.

"Then I won't go."

"Why not?"

"That will leave Adolf alone all day."

Verian shrugged. "So what? Happens a lot. He likes it. He gets tired of all of us fussing."

"I'll talk to him," Renata said, and turned to go.

Verian said, "Wait, look here," and turned

to open the refrigerator door. "There's his lunch. There's his morning snack and his afternoon snack. Here's his insulin. I refilled his prescription not long ago, he gives himself his shots when he comes down for breakfast at eight. He'll be okay, Renata. Go fishing. Just see that you bring home enough for tomorrow's dinner and leave the guy alone."

While Verian cooked breakfast for the family and himself, Renata went to talk to Adolf anyway and got pretty much the same response.

"You're sure you'll be all right?"

"Look, Renata, Uncle Verian always takes a couple of days off every month, and I do like being alone."

She was still upstairs when Verian called up, "Phone, Renata." It was Bart.

"Look, hon, Dad has this remodeling job he needs a little help with. It will take at least an hour and that will make us late getting started. Do you want to put this off for another day?"

"I was just thinking that maybe I should," Renata said.

Verian took the phone from her. "Go fishing," he said to Bart, and explained Renata's reluctance.

"Tell her I'll be there around nine," Bart said and hung up.

It was ten o'clock before Bart cleared the yacht harbor channel and had the whaler out in the open sea. It was a twenty-footer with a small cabin amidship. Bart cut the big motor and drifted while they baited troll lines with anchovy and let them out over the stern. The Channel Islands were dim grey outlines through thinning fog as they began to make slow headway north following the coastline about three miles out.

Renata stood in the cockpit looking back at the receding town of Port Haven. A month, she said to herself, a whole month. It was hard to believe, and of course, it couldn't last. The wonder was that it had lasted this long, doubtless because coming home was the last thing expected of her. It had been long enough for the estate to be transferred to her, and that would give her more options.

The town was what you might find pictured in a travel folder, Renata thought, with many white-walled houses with red tiled roofs filling a shallow basin and climbing up the lower ridges of Padre Mountain. She had never loved it more than she did today. She would like to stay—wanted to stay. There must be some way . . . Now, she thought, there was also Bart.

Renata turned to look at Bart, and he patted the seat beside him where he sat at the wheel. They were making less than five knots on the small motor.

"In a minute," she said, "after we're beyond Promontory Point and I can't see the town any more."

He laughed. "I forgot. You always did that."

"I guess I did," Renata said. "I'd forgotten too. It's such a pretty place."

They were beyond the point now, so she went to sit beside him. He put his arms around her, and she didn't resist, but she didn't cuddle. She asked him about the remodeling job and they talked for a while.

They took in the lines and rebaited the hooks long before they reached Santa Barbara, and had one rock cod and a surfer shark. Bart removed the hook from the shark's mouth and tossed it over the side. They returned to the cabin, and as Renata watched the shoreline slide slowly past, she said, "I own that," pointing to a small stretch of shoreline between two streams that emptied into the ocean.

"What?" Bart turned to look.

"I own that," Renata repeated. "The probate closed and I signed the last papers a few days ago. That belonged to Dad, and now it's mine."

Bart said, "Great Jehovah! You're sure, Renata?"

"Yes, I'm sure. Mr. Silas showed me on a map. There are a few other parcels, but he said that was the best."

Bart laughed. "The taxes on it must have been a bundle."

"The taxes were a bundle, but I didn't pay much attention to the itemized statement. There was a certified audit and a lot of other stuff. Mr. Silas said the zoning was favorable for the inheritance tax appraisal."

Bart laughed. "Renata, you're going to have to learn about property values. How many acres are in the parcel?"

"It's not very big . . . a little less than ten acres."

"Holy cow-" Bart said. "Ten acres with a minimum of four hundred feet of waterfront. Woman, you're rich. And I was thinking of asking you to marry me!"

Renata turned from looking at the shoreline to face Bart. What she saw in those mild blue eyes was not hot, demanding passion, but tenderness and caring. For the rest of her life she could have that—for the rest of her life.

"I didn't mean for it to come out like that," Bart said. "I thought I'd wait until we anchored somewhere to eat lunch."

Renata laughed and leaned over to kiss him. The kiss turned out to be more than casual, after which Bart cut the throttle, letting them drift, and took her into his arms while he did a thorough job of letting her know what it was like to be properly kissed by a man in love. Her response seemed to be totally satisfactory to Bart, and to her surprise, stirred her to a point where she felt they had better back off.

She stayed in his arms for a moment while she thought about this stirring of her emotions. On the whole she felt quite happy about it, not just because she could feel like this, but because it had given her pleasure to give him pleasure. They had told her that would be important. *It's okay*, Renata told herself. *I'm okay*, and sighed with a deep contentment. Then Bart began kissing her again, his hands moving over her body. For a moment she went rigid. His hands ceased to move, they cradled her, and then he broke away as the catch on the reel sounded. They had a strike! They looked at each other and laughed, and hurried to tend the lines.

While they worked, Bart said, "I suppose you've already guessed, but I love you."

While Renata helped pull in the halibut caught while they drifted, she laughed with a happiness she had lost all hope of knowing. "I love you too, Bart."

Russell Revolo was the first to enter the Riff house that evening. He came in just before six. The house was quiet—very quiet. Russell hung his topcoat in the entry hall closet and went into the living room to mix himself his usual drink. Renata was supposed to be taking Verian's place in the kitchen. Drink in hand, he went to see. The kitchen gleamed with Verian's usual neatness. Russell opened the refrigerator door. Afolf's lunch was there under a plastic cover, as was a plate of snacks. Russell closed the refrigerator and looked in the sink. One salad plate, the size Verian used for Adolf's snacks.

In the trash basket under the sink, Russell found the disposable hypodermic syringe Adolf used to give himself insulin shots and an empty insulin vial. He was careful not to touch either. Russell straightened and stood looking out the kitchen window while his mind considered possibilities, then he went upstairs.

Adolf's long, thin body was stretched out on the bedroom floor. His head was toward the door. There was vomit on the rug. Russell knelt down, bending near Adolf's face. Adolf was breathing deeply, very deeply, and there was a strong smell of acetone. He placed his fingers on the cold wrist, but could get no pulse. Russell had not lived in the house with a diabetic for years without knowing the symptoms of diabetic coma. He hurried to the phone and called Dr. Craig, asking for instructions.

Det. Sergeant Mike Wiley knocked on the open door of Captain Ed Staple's office. It was ten o'clock on Thursday morning.

"Captain," Mike said, "Russell Revolo is in the outer office. Adolf Riff died last night. Mr. Revolo suspects foul play. He wants to talk to you about a missing vial of insulin."

6

Seeing Russell Revolo only reinforced Ed's recollection of a shrewd and cunning dandy. Russell's tanned handsome face wore a suitably somber expression as he entered the office and extended a soft-fleshed hand toward Ed.

"We've met," Russell said. "You bought an antique corner cupboard from me, if you remember."

Ed acknowledged that he remembered, expressed his satisfaction with his purchase, and offered his regrets over Adolf Riff's death. After extracting his hand from Russell's clinging grasp, Ed invited his guest to sit down. Mike slipped into his accustomed place in the corner of the room.

"Sgt. Wiley tells me you have reason to suspect foul play in the death of Adolf Riff.

Please, tell me about it, Mr. Revolo, and who it is you suspect."

Russell's eyebrows raised as he regarded Ed with "grave concern" through brown eyes fringed with long, thick lashes.

"Well, Captain Staple, I wouldn't like to make an accusation of any one person at this point. I thought you would make an investigation and then an arrest—provided, of course, I'm right and Adolf's death wasn't what it seems."

Russell, Ed thought, was a little much. His looks were too perfect, his manner too sober, his smile too sincere. Ed had the feeling that he was about to take part in a charade: ask the right question, get the next clue.

"You have suspicions of this but no proof, is that it?"

"Yes, Captain," Russell nodded and smiled. "That's it exactly."

"What aroused your suspicion, Mr. Revolo?"

"The missing insulin vial. Adolf has been diabetic since childhood—since birth, probably, but he has maintained reasonable health with medication and diet. None of us expected he would die for many years yet."

"By none of us, you mean yourself and . . . ?"

He seemed to be on track so far, Ed thought.

"My wife, Audrey, Verian Riff, Adolf's uncle, and I suppose his sister, Renata. You know Renata, I believe. At her insistence

67

Adolf was recently hospitalized overnight to undergo tests by a specialist. The findings confirmed the family doctor's diagnosis. Adolf suffered from diabetes and periodic palpitations of the heart. No change was made in his medication. The specialist merely confirmed what we all knew."

"Yet in spite of all indications to the contrary, Adolf Riff died last night and that set you to wondering why."

"Yes," Russell nodded, his expression again showing grave concern. "Exactly."

"Mr. Revolo, I can understand the shock of sudden death and your concern, but you must know that it is not at all unusual for terminally ill persons to have a period when they seem much improved just preceding death."

Russell sighed and sank back in his chair in obvious dejection. "I wish I could believe that was true in this case, but there *is* a missing insulin vial and Adolf had gone into diabetic coma when I came home and found him yesterday evening."

Ed searched his memory for some knowledge of what the significance of this discovery might mean, but could only recall that diabetics went into coma from insufficient insulin. A missing vial implied others, so insulin would be available.

Ed said, "Mr. Revolo, we are totally unfamiliar with the circumstances surrounding Mr. Riff's death. How do you connect the missing vial with that event?"

Once again Ed felt that he had asked the right question as Russell straightened, his expression becoming alert, ready to cooperate, although not quite eager.

"Adolf gave himself his insulin injections. The vial must have been tampered with, otherwise he would have been all right for the day." Russell nodded encouragingly. "Do you understand?"

"Not completely," Ed said. "Perhaps you had better begin with when the injection was administered, and the events that followed, in chronological order if possible."

With very little help, Russell outlined the ordinary daily routine of the Riff household, and the extraordinary events of the day of Adolf's death. When he had finished, Ed had agreed to investigate the circumstances surrounding the missing insulin vial, and Russell, properly resolute at having done his sorrowful duty, after giving Ed's hand a meaningful squeeze, left the office at ten-thirty.

Mike moved to occupy the chair where Russell had been sitting. He waited, giving Ed time to think through the interview. Mike noted that today, Ed's vest matched his navy jacket. The captain wasn't feeling restless.

"What do you think?" Mike asked Ed.

Ed leaned back until his chair creaked and smiled at Mike.

"If I read my clues right, then it seems the subject we were acting out was: Renata killed her brother. Do you agree?"

Mike nodded. "Russell must have known Renata visited you and guessed why. Adolf dies. Renata is the last person to see him alive, then is gone all day. Russell comes home and sizes up the situation. Opportunity has knocked. It's a sweet frame with little trouble on his part. He comes to you knowing that you, being the smart cop you are, with a bit of help will see through Renata's story of mortal jeopardy, and presto!"

Mike spread his hands in an expansive gesture.

"I was wondering," Ed said as he turned his chair so that he looked out his west window, "what do you suppose we would have thought if Renata hadn't come to us first?"

"We'd have listened. It smells frame, but we might have gone about it a little differently."

"Such as?"

"We might have let him know he would be a heavy suspect himself to see if he'd back off."

"Do you think he would have?"

"Nope. I think he's playing the cards he was dealt. What does he have to lose?"

Ed nodded agreement as he swung away from the window to face Mike.

"I think we'd better have an autopsy," Ed said. "You phone the mortuary and tell them what we want. I'll get the medical examiner. Then we'll visit the next of kin and see if we can get permission."

* * *

"Why?" Renata asked. "Why an autopsy when Dr. Craig was present at the time of death and has already signed the death certificate? Adolf died of natural causes, ask Dr. Craig."

"We will, but in the meantime, there are questions only an autopsy can answer. Since the question has been raised, I think you would be wise to grant the request, Miss Riff. It is the only way to establish the truth."

They were standing in the Riff living room, a long room with a fireplace at one end and a square bay window at the other. It had been luxuriously carpeted, possibly over old oak flooring, Ed thought. Comfortable seating in several groupings were scattered among antiques that made him long to examine them closely. Renata turned and walked to the bay window.

For a few moments she did not allow any thought to enter her mind. Then she breathed deeply and sighed. Poor Adolf, how could she do this to him? What had Adolf ever done to anybody? He had been a nice, sweet, gentle soul all his life. He had never been anything but kind and generous to Russell. *Russell*, that devil. It was easy to see that he planned to frame her for Adolf's death. Renata wondered, could he make it work? She wouldn't care so much except that now there was Bart.

Renata closed her eyes against a sudden welling up of totally unaccustomed tears.

When had she cried last? But Bart . . . So much happiness so near, and she dare not claim it. So, what did it matter?

Renata didn't turn back to face Ed when she answered. Her voice was low, the words clear. "All right, have your autopsy. Maybe it will be best after all. There are things I wonder about also."

She turned, her eyes holding that fierce light, her small body rigid with anger.

"Don't forget, Captain Staple, what I came to see you about in the first place."

Ed nodded and smiled, then, when she began to move toward them, he spoke.

"Thank you, Miss Riff. I wonder if you would be kind enough to call the mortuary to tell them you have given your consent."

She paused, her eyelids narrowing, her lips opening as if in protest, and Ed feared she would change her mind. She didn't speak, but with an exasperated sigh, she crossed the room to enter the little alcove off the central hall where Alva's French style phone rested on a built-in desk.

When she returned, Ed said, "If it's all right, Detective Wiley will call our office from here, then if your uncle is at home we'd like to speak with him . . . Verian, isn't it?"

Renata waved a hand in permission, then sank into the blue damask chair that had been her mother's favorite.

"Go ahead," she said. "Uncle Verian is in the kitchen. He'd probably prefer talking to you there."

* * *

The interview with Verian had been interesting, if not very productive. Verian, for whatever reasons, was hedging his bets. His time schedule for the previous day tallied with Russell's. Yes, he had expected the "boy" to live for many more years. No, he wasn't all that surprised, only saddened; he had loved that boy.

Yes, there was an insulin vial missing. It was a multi-dose vial, and Adolf should have emptied it at eight o'clock when he gave himself his morning injection. Yes, he had the prescription refilled as needed. He did all the household buying and the cooking.

Of course, he had made a search of the inside and outside trash receptacles, and had searched Adolf's room, but had not found the empty vial. Sure they could send their own men over—if it was okay with Renata, she owned the place now.

Mike had done the questioning, and when he had gotten all he thought he could, he gave a sidelong look toward the front of the house, and dropping his tone of voice to a confidential level, asked, "You don't suppose old Craig made a mistake, do you? I mean, he treated Adolf for years, but he's getting up there in age."

Verian had given Mike a look that clearly said, *You can't sucker me.*

"Better men than Craig have made mistakes," Verian said, "and there's that specialist Renata insisted on dragging Adolf to see. He agreed with Craig right down the line."'

Verian had turned back to his cooking, and they returned to Renata. Ed had decided questioning her could wait. It wasn't always wise to push too hard. Better to give her a little breather. Better to talk with the others and maybe save her until the autopsy report came in. Ed thanked her for her cooperation, asked permission to have the seach made for the missing vial, then said good-bye.

Ed stood on the curb and looked back at the old house before he got in the car. It had recently been painted a pleasing soft slate blue with white on the cornices, tall window facings, and the posts and railings of the porches. The front facade was narrow, the height exceeding the width. The hip roof had been cropped to accommodate a white railed captain's walk, with access, Ed guessed, through the cupola, a bit of whimsy in white with a whale weathervane on top.

His glance traveled down from the tin whale to the windows of the third floor. Her room would be there, in the worst possible location for her safety. Verian doubtless occupied quarters in the lean-to kitchen wing, and the Revolos' rooms would be on the second floor of the house.

Movement from the front bay window caught his attention. Renata stood there. Ed raised his hand in a salute, smiled, and got into the car.

"We'll go talk with Dr. Craig," Ed said as Mike pulled away from the curb.

Dr. Hiram Craig, wearing his white office coat with his stethoscope around his neck, came into his small office where Ed and Mike waited and sat down in the chair behind the desk. He blew out a long sigh.

"You're here about Adolf Riff, I suppose," Craig said.

"Yes, sir," Ed said. "You were his physician and you were present at his death. Is that true?"

"Yes. Death was due to natural causes. He died as the result of uncontrolled diabetes, complicated by congenital heart disease. Hard to separate the two in this case."

"You made tests after he was admitted to the hospital in a state of diabetic coma, Doctor?"

"Of course," Craig nodded. "The results were as expected. Blood tests showed his glucose up, carbon dioxide down, and ketones in the plasma. The urine tests showed glucose up and ketones up. He had been in a coma for several hours."

"How many, at a guess?"

"At a guess, since noon, five or six at least. Too long. We couldn't pull him out of it with his heart condition. Heart went into ventricular fibrillation. Couldn't get it back into sinus rhythm."

"For your findings would you say Mr. Riff had failed to take his morning insulin? That was normally at eight o'clock wasn't it?"

"Yes. Eight at the latest. If he overslept, Verian had had orders to wake him. I would say he took his morning injection, definitely."

Ed said, "If Mr. Riff had given himself his usual dosage of insulin as you've said, would you have expected him to go into coma by noon, Dr. Craig?"

Craig looked at Ed questioningly, through half-closed lids. "No, not ordinarily."

"However, you are satisfied he died of natural causes. Is that true, Doctor?"

Craig pushed back his chair, studying Ed solemnly before replying.

"I signed the death certificate to that effect. Yes."

Ed let a little time elapse. Craig remained still, watching him.

"Hypothetically," Ed said, "if Mr. Riff had failed to get his morning insulin, or if the vial had been tampered with, how long before coma would ensue?"

"Possibly by ten o'clock, Captain Staple. But Adolf did take his injection. He took it in the presence of his sister, Renata. She assured me of that. She gave him the vial herself and watched while he administered the insulin."

7

"I'm glad you came early," Renata said to Bart. "Russell will be here soon and I want to keep out of his way. Let's go up to the cupola where we can have some privacy."

As they climbed the stairs, Renata told Bart about Ed Staple's visit and the autopsy. In the third floor hall, Bart stood in front of the door that concealed the circular staircase to the cupola while he looked down at Renata.

"You're telling me Russell has accused you of murdering Adolf? Is that what you're saying?"

Looking up at him, Renata thought the blue eyes were not so gentle now. His face told her he was struggling between disbelief and anger. Yesterday wasn't just a wonderful dream. He did love her. Her spirits soared. If only . . . ! If only . . . !

"Oh, he didn't make a formal accusation, but he must have something to base his actions on other than a wild hope."

"You mean he framed you?" Bart put his hands on her shoulders while he looked at her keenly, searching her face as if to be sure he had heard correctly. She shrugged.

"And he's still living here? You haven't thrown the bastard out? Well . . ."

"Don't get worked up, Bart. If I threw him out it would look like guilt."

Renata gave a little dry laugh. "He probably figures this is his best shot. Now that Adolf's gone, he knows he won't be living here long, and that makes it harder to arrange for my accidental death. To frame me for murder is much simpler under the circumstances. I suppose I shouldn't have been surprised. He had to give it a try."

Bart's lips set in a firm straight line of determination. "You're pretty cool about this, Renata. I think you should tell him to go now, no matter how it would *look*. I'll do it for you, if you'd like."

"No. It's better this way. I can keep tabs on him. Besides, there are things I wonder about."

"It's dangerous."

"I know, but Captain Staple isn't going to be taken in. Let's let him handle it, shall we?"

Bart opened the door and followed Renata up the tight circle of stairs. They emerged through a trap door in the center of the cupola and stood for a moment looking over the panorama of Refugio Bay and the Pacific Ocean. In the early twilight the Channel Islands were grey shapes on the horizon. In a few minutes the sun would slip behind a cloud bank and after a while the afterglow would tint the whole world a roseate hue. Bart turned from the view, his arms going around Renata. She lifted her face for his kiss.

"I love you, Bart," Renata said, "and I don't want to give you up."

"You couldn't lose me if you tried," he said, and kissed her again.

"Look here, Renata," Bart said. "I had planned to court you, not too long, but I wanted to enjoy all the fun we missed. Now that things have changed so, I don't think we should wait. I think we should get married as soon as possible. You don't seem to be taking this very seriously, but damn it, you should. He's bound to have something cooked up, why else would there be an autopsy? Craig was present when Adolf died, there's no reason . . ."

Renata interrupted, "The autopsy will doubtless substantiate Craig's opinion. It's being done so there can't be any future questions raised. I hated giving permission for it, but Staple was right. It was the only thing to do."

She paused and chose a seat on the built-in bench of the cupola, pulling him down beside her.

"It's not the autopsy that worries me, it's the time it will take, plus the investigation is bound to make the papers. I had hoped for a quiet, quick funeral, but now I'll have to notify all the relatives. We aren't a close family, but everybody comes for funerals and weddings. It destroys my anonymity, Bart. I'm afraid it will lead to trouble."

"What kind of trouble?"

"I may have to leave very quickly."

"Why?"

She was silent, her eyes raised to study his face, her hands holding his with a desperate strength.

Bart smiled and touched her cheek. "Look, darling, we'll deal with the past when we must, but for now forget all that, we've got to handle the present. I don't think you realize how serious this is or what's at stake. I don't know just how he intends to get his hands on it, but Russell must know you've inherited a gold mine. That piece of property you showed me up the coast, Renata, the land alone is worth a million as raw land."

She released his hands and sat back to look off up the coast, in the general direction of the beach property.

"A million?"

"Yes, and I suppose there are other parcels."

"Well, yes, there are, but . . ."

"Renata," Bart said, "Verian is bound to be in this. They mean to get you. I can't let you fight them alone."

She was sitting very still, hardly breathing. She'd had no idea the stakes were so high. She should think about this.

"All right. I'll give Russell a time limit. I can't do anything about Uncle Verian, but that will break them up."

Bart took her hands in his, they were cold. "Renata . . ." he began, but was interrupted by a voice from below. It was Verian calling up to tell Renata that her Aunt Consuella from Santa Barabara was on the phone.

"It has started," Renata said. "I'll have to go. Kiss me once more, Bart, and tell me you love me."

Ed Staple did the prescribed forty laps in his pool, toweled off, and went inside. The County Coroner's Office was at the county seat, so he hadn't expected immediate results, but this was Tuesday. Even counting the weekend he should have had something. The body of Adolf Riff had been released to his family. Burial had been Monday. Ed had attended, along with Mike. They'd been surprised at the number of people who came to see Adolf laid to rest.

While he waited for the autopsy reports, Ed had visited John Silas and come away more surprised at the extent of the Riff estate, Adolf's disposition of his personal fortune, and his understanding of both his illness and the people close to him. Ed had talked again with both Russell and Verian, and had a telephone conversation with the county medical examiner. After a long talk with the specialist who saw Adolf at Renata's insistence, he had put Mike to work gathering information.

Tuesdays Suzanna cooked Mexican. Tonight it was chicken enchiladas with fried rice and refried beans. The sauce was hot and spicy. There was a side dish of guacamole and another of sour cream to cool the palate, along with sliced tomatoes and hearts of lettuce to please his American taste. Dessert was a honeyed squash with whipped cream.

The weather had turned cool with a promise of rain, making the fire on his small hearth seem doubly pleasant while he enjoyed his after-dinner cigar and brandy. Ed watched the flames through the haze of his cigar smoke and, feeling perfectly relaxed, asked himself why he was sitting here instead of working off Suzanna's high calorie meal with an attractive girl. An evening in a disco wouldn't hurt him. His back would stand it, and going out would quash Suzanna's insinuations that he was getting serious about Jamie.

For a few minutes he reviewed his possibilities. Tonight, somehow, their images seemed to fade and in the end it was Renata who stayed in his thoughts. However, Ed's interest in her wasn't as a possible companion for the evening. He was, Ed thought, a little awed by Renata, there was so much hidden. She had a quick intelligence and she toyed with danger, coolly, knowingly moving pieces about as if she played a familiar game of checkers.

Here he was, back at the Riff case again. Once again, Ed reviewed possible dates, then admitted, even to quiet Suzanna's little knowing remarks, he wasn't going out.

From the table beside him, Ed picked up a new catalog from one of the antique auctions he attended. There might possibly be a duck decoy or two he could afford, since there had been a substantial windfall from the Coachella Valley farm. They had caught the market this year.

The telephone rang. Ed swirled the last swig of brandy in his glass, savored the aroma, swallowed the aromatic liquid, and caught the call on the fifth ring.

"Staple." Ed recognized the crisp, staccato tones of the county medical examiner. "Had to be in Port Haven today. Stopped by to see my old friend Hiram Craig. About that question you asked. There's a possibility you may be right. Not a chance in hell of proving it. Besides, what would be the motive? Craig says Adolf's death cuts Verian off from the Riff estate."

"If I'm right," Ed said, "this whole business hinges on Renata's homecoming throwing some well laid plans out of kilter. If Verian had been tampering with Adolf's medication, it was after Alva's death and before Renata's return. That would explain her concern for Adolf's rapid deterioration. I think Verian had gone too far and time and circumstances took over. Had Craig noticed anything during that time span?''

''Yes, but nothing more than might be expected. He changed the medication to meet the need, but the incidences of fibrillation continued to increase. Really no timetable for these things. Depends on the individual. Craig did what he could.''

''That's about what I expected,'' Ed said. ''Thanks, Doc. Now what about the autopsy?''

''Nothing there. Wouldn't be, considering the time lapse. Nothing showed other than the medication Craig administered at the hospital. All very proper. Death due to natural causes. Heart muscle badly deteriorated. Can't say he wasn't helped along. Can't prove it either way. That's the short of it. Full report on your desk tomorrow.''

Ed poured another two fingers of brandy, selected another cigar, and got out the auction catalog, but his thoughts soon drifted to the Riff case.

To begin with, the missing insulin vial hadn't been found. Ed wondered what bit of hocus pocus would be pulled when that became necessary—assuming the case hung on that bit of evidence. It was no good setting up the assumption that Renata had conveniently let it drop over the side of the Boston whaler. There had to be something more, something provable against her. What?

Why, Ed asked himself was he sitting here mulling over this obviously contrived case?

He exhaled blue smoke and sipped his brandy and recalled the dream where Renata caught the fish with his face. She had him hooked all right, just like the fish in the dream.

Ed put down his cigar and his brandy snifter, went to the phone and dialed. A voice with a pleasant, lilting cadence answered.

"Jamie," Ed said. Let Suzanna think what she would.

Russell, in mauve silk pajamas and robe, knocked at Verian's door. Verian's apartment had originally been the servants' quarters. There had been a sitting room, two small bedrooms and a bath. The two bedrooms had been knocked into one and the whole refurnished soon after Verian came to live in his brother Augustin's home. In the years since, Verian had added his own touches, so that the room Russell entered showed a man of simple fastidious taste, with a love of horses and fresh air. The room was too cool for Russell, the chairs of Danish modern, although comfortable, lacked the elegance of velvet and down that Russell preferred. No matter, he didn't plan to stay long.

"You wanted to talk with me," Russell said.

"You'd better believe I want to talk to you."

Verian closed the door behind Russell and returned to his chair of sculptured blond wood with cushions and foot rest covered in brown suede. He pushed a button on the remote control and the TV screen went to black.

"Sit down." Verian indicated another chair, a black wooden framework supporting a sling-type seat of beige leather.

"Staple been to see you?" Verian asked.

Russell nodded. "He dropped by the office and took me to lunch. Didn't have much to say. What did he want with you?"

"Mostly to let me know he smelled a rat, I guess. This thing's gone sour, Russell. I think we should back off. I told you you didn't have enough to go to court."

Russell shifted in his chair. Verian really did keep this room too cool. "Has Staple talked with *her* yet?"

"Nope. Saving her for after the autopsy report, I guess."

"Well, if everything you told me is right, she should pretty well incriminate herself."

"I'm telling you, Russell, it's not enough. Staple's no fool and neither is Mike Wiley."

Russell's eyes narrowed and his fingers began to drum out his irritation on the wooden chair arms.

"Well, maybe it is a long shot, but it's all we've got right now."

"There are other ways."

"Such as?"

"What's wrong with the original plan?"

"The neat little accident or the possible suicide?" Russell gave a derisive snort. "Forget it. She's taken care of that. Unless you want to do it yourself."

"Uh-uh, no way I'm going to give Renata a push down the stairs."

Russell's smile was more than half sneer.

"Very touching," he said. "Your sentiments didn't keep you from helping Adolf out of this world and into the next."

Verian grinned. "Different matter," he said. "The boy wasn't long for this world and I'm not getting any younger. I want to enjoy the years I have left. Understand?"

"Perfectly. I have a few plans of my own."

"Then you'd better come up with something that will work."

Russell's fingers drummed on the chair arms, then grew still, and his eyes took on a pleased expression.

"If this fails," he said, "there's Tanner."

"No." Verian's head turned sharply, his lips setting in a firm, hard line.

"Why not? A word in the right place and little Renata would be gone." Russell bunched his fingertips together, pressed them to his lips and blew them away.

"Her and her fortune with her," Verian said. "No. I won't go for that. Not Tanner . . . No."

"I'll leave you out of it. I'll do it."

"Death is one thing, Russell, but there's things that are worse. The minute I hear you've put out the word, I'll go to her with the truth. Anyway, I reckon he'll probably get wind of her whereabouts soon enough what with the funeral and all the stuff in the papers. But he won't kill her, not Tanner."

Russell gave Verian a long, hard look. Lord, this room was like an igloo.

"Close that window, Verian," Russell said. "I'm freezing."

Verian chuckled and went to close the window.

"Well, what are we going to do?"

Russell hugged himself, rubbing his arms with his hands. "Maybe we could rig it so Tanner took the blame."

"Frame Tanner? You've gone nuts."

"Look here, Verian, there's a fortune in property at stake. We made a deal. You inherit and I manage the estate. I want that deal."

"Then it's up to you."

"I can't do it alone. I'll be out of this house after Sunday, and there's no way Renata will stand for so much as a social visit. I'm lucky she gave me a week."

Both men were silent, staring at each other.

"It will work," Russell said, "if everything you told me is right, it'll work."

"If it doesn't . . . ?"

"I'll think of something. *I'll think of something.*"

"It had better be fast, before Tanner does catch up with her."

8

Mike Wiley paused before entering Ed's office. When Ed looked up from reading the autopsy report on Adolf Riff, Mike went in.

"Have you seen this?" Ed asked.

"No, sir."

Mike took the chair beside the desk, accepted the report, and began to read. When he had finished, Ed told him of the conversation with the county medical examiner, commenting that it was about as expected, and it was now time to have a talk with Renata.

"Here, or there, do you think?" Ed said.

"Who's still in the house?" Mike asked.

"They all are, so far as I know."

"Then here, Captain. Russell and his wife should be at work, but Verian can't be counted on to stay in the kitchen."

Ed nodded, reached for the phone, looked at Mike, and waited. Mike told him the number from memory and Ed dialed. The conversation was brief.

"She'll be here in half an hour," Ed said as he picked up a report on a new case which they discussed until Mike went downstairs to meet Renata and escort her upstairs.

Ed had told Jamie about the Riff case and Jamie had said, "if it bothers you, turn it over to Mike. He's surely capable of handling it, or do you feel obligated because she came in asking for you personally?"

Ed had been forced to think that over, and the answer he gave Jamie amounted to no answer at all. He had said he supposed his feeling for the case was a holdover from the days when an officer assigned to a case followed it through from beginning to end. Jamie had laughed softly.

"Certainly that's very commendable,"she had said. Then, as if to reward him, she had stood, put down her drink, and after looking kindly at him for a moment, pulled him to his feet and led him into the bedroom. It was the first time she had taken any kind of initiative in their relationship.

As he usually did, Mike knocked at the open office door before standing aside to announce Renata. Mike felt the ritual had the effect of Ed granting an audience.

Renata's smile held a touch of mischief as

she said, "Good morning, Captain. Detective Wiley tells me you now have the autopsy report."

Ed stood until Renata was seated across from him and Mike had taken his usual corner seat, then he handed Renata the report.

"A lot of gobble-de-gook," she said, after she had glanced at it. "Just tell me about it."

Ed gave her the information, then said, "Now, Miss Riff, would you take me through the events of that morning, beginning with the approximate time you entered the kitchen to get the lunch basket Verian had packed. I realize almost a week has passed, but your best recollection, please."

Renata talked, Ed listened, and Mike wrote in the small notebook he carried.

Presently, Ed asked, "Was it while Verian and the Revolos ate breakfast that you went up to talk with Adolf?"

"Yes. He insisted that I go fishing as planned."

"When you came back downstairs the Revolos and Verian were still in the breakfast room until the Revolos left for work. You were alone in the kitchen until Adolf came down. Is that correct?"

"Yes."

"When Adolf came downstairs, Verian gave him his orange juice. At that time the doorbell rang and Verian went to meet the friend who was his companion for the day. That was . . . ?"

Renata shrugged. "After eight, say eight-ten or twelve."

"You took Adolf's insulin and hypodermic syringe from the refrigerator and watched him give himself the usual morning injection."

"Not exactly. I watched him fill the syringe. It was the last of the multi-dose vial. But I could never watch the actual injection."

"All right, then Adolf disposed of the vial and the syringe. How?"

"I threw them both in the trash."

Ed very carefully kept his face expressionless. "How many vials were there?"

Renate moved restlessly. "In the refrigerator? Four or five."

"You are sure Adolf emptied the vial he used?"

"He said, 'That's the last of that one.' They're multi-dose vials. I think that's the term. Why?"

"You handled the vial twice, is that correct?"

"Yes."

"After Adolf returned to his room, you tidied up the kitchen. Is that true?"

"When Verian had served Adolf's breakfast, I told him to go on and to take Mother's Mercedes. He and Dad Schooner were delighted and left the house joking about the effect that would have on their friends."

"After Adolf left the kitchen, you never saw him again?"

"Oh, yes."

"You went to say good-bye?"

"Yes. He had begun work on his book."

"He said nothing to you except good-bye?"

"He said, 'Don't worry. I'll be all right.' I asked if he had his digitalis. He said no, his pillbox was empty, he would have to get more from the supply Verian kept in the kitchen. I refilled the pillbox and returned it to him."

"He physically took it from you?"

"Yes," Renata said sharply. She was growing irritated.

"Just a couple more questions," Ed said and smiled.

"Adolf took the pillbox from you, and you left him."

"No. I filled his water carafe."

"You wanted to make sure he would have his digitalis and the water with which to take it."

She nodded.

"And then you left?"

"Bart honked from the street. I waved to him from the front window in Adolf's room, then kissed my brother good-bye and left the house. What is this, Captain Staple, the inquisition?"

She had been relaxed and cooperative, but had turned defensive. He would have to move quickly.

He smiled at her. "In a way. Part of the job."

Ed waited, letting her grow calm, letting her assurance rebuild.

"According to Dr. Craig, Adolf had not

responded favorably to recent changes in his medication. Only Verian handled that medication. You were aware of that, I believe."

"Of course."

She was definitely defensive now, and not only for herself. "You were concerned enough about Adolf's condition to consult a specialist. Isn't that correct?"

"He confirmed Dr. Craig's diagnosis."

"Did the specialist tell you that Adolf's condition was very unstable and extreme care should be exercised in the amount and balance of both the insulin and the digitalis?"

"Yes. I told you, he confirmed Dr. Craig's diagnosis. He did not change the medication."

"Did you, Miss Riff? Did you alter the medication on that morning, knowing that to do so could be fatal to your brother?"

Renata was on her feet, staring in absolute disbelief. The fierce look came back into her eyes and the pretty sensuous line of her lips straightened into grim firmness. She breathed deeply and exhaled through slightly parted lips.

"Are you accusing me of murdering my brother, Captain Staple?"

Ed returned her fiery gaze with calm seriousness. "I'm asking you a very logical question under the circumstances, Miss Riff, so sit down."

She was slow to comply and Ed waited until she had.

"You personally placed both the digitalis and the insulin in your brother's hands. Were they, to the best of your knowledge and belief, as prescribed by Dr. Craig?"

"Yes."

"Did you in any way alter the amounts of medication given him that morning?"

"No." She snapped the word, then added. "Why should I?"

"Well, Miss Riff, although you have complete control of your inheritance, Russell Revolo had control of Adolf. Had he lived, it would soon have been necessary to institutionalize Adolf. Were you aware of this?"

"The specialist and Dr. Craig told me what to expect."

"John Silas informed you, didn't he, that during your absence, Adolf, aware that this was inevitable, had caused documents to be executed making Russell Revolo his guardian. That meant that in providing for your brother, after his transfer to institutional care, you would be forced to deal with Russell."

"So?" Renata, still angrily defiant, shrugged. "That could easily have been handled through the courts."

"I believe you had expressed your intention of forcing the Revolos to move out as soon as the estate was settled."

Renata gave a derisive laugh. "I relented at Adolf's request, but now I have given them until Sunday, which I thought extremely generous."

Ed smiled. "I understand, and approve. But, Miss Riff, what I want you to understand is, given the facts as stated, a capable attorney could present a credible case. The district attorney could be persuaded to bring charges against you."

Renata laughed, not hysterically, but with ironic amusement. "Captain Staple, I can't believe you are serious and I will submit to no more of this."

She pushed back her chair and stood. "You needn't see me out, Detective Wiley. I know the way," Renata said and was gone.

There was silence in the office while Ed and Mike exchanged satisfied glances. Presently, Ed leaned back in his chair.

"You have the report from the pharmacy and the run-down on Verian's friends?"

"Yes, sir."

"Then I guess that's it. We can get them all together. Tonight, would you say, after the Revolos are at home?"

Mike nodded. "No need to wait."

Ed stood on the curb looking at the Riff house. Maybe some day, he thought, he would have an opportunity to wander through the whole structure leisurely, examining the antiques; family pieces all of them, some from whaling days and China trade.

Mike moved on ahead and Ed followed. Six o'clock, time to get on with it.

They were in the living room, scattered about, with Renata at the bay window, the Revolos in chairs on opposite sides of the fireplace, and Verian in a club chair with a Chinese black lacquer, ivory inlaid cabinet and a silver based lamp beside it.

Ed took a moment to study Audrey Revolo. She had a round, flat face with large blue eyes made larger by the heavy lenses of her glasses. Her hair was brown, simply cut to below her ears, and shining clean. She met his glance, but behind the calm, Ed read fear. An intelligent, thoroughly capable, conservative sort of woman, Ed thought, blindly loyal to her suave, handsome husband.

When Russell had made the introduction, Ed smiled at her reassuringly, and said, "There is no need for Mrs. Revolo to stay for this."

Audrey said, "I don't mind," but when Ed rearranged them, using the sofa grouping along the long wall, he saw Russell touch her arm and say the single word, "Go." Audrey hesitated, but then quietly slipped from the room.

"I'll get right on with this," Ed began, and with a few sentences stated the circumstances and brought the situation up to the autopsy report. Mike handed each of them a copy.

"In many ways, this case has been unusual and I have departed from normal procedure on more than one occasion, as I am doing now in giving you this report," Ed said. "I do this to aid any of you who may want to seek further advice."

Mike had returned to his chair, but Ed still hesitated.

"According to the medical men consulted in this case," he began, "Adolf Riff's disease —both diabetes and congestive heart failure —followed the usual pattern for such chronic disorders until approximately six months ago, when Adolf's heart began to fail more rapidly. Not alarmingly, but Adolf did not respond well to changes in his medication. Dr. Craig considered recommending institutionalizing Adolf, but hoped to postpone that step until after Christmas. When Miss Riff returned, became alarmed, and insisted on consulting a specialist, Craig delayed mentioning his plans. You all know the results."

Ed paused while Russell and Verian exchanged glances, but as neither of them spoke, Ed continued.

"At Adolf's sudden death, Mr. Revolo, perhaps because he had been so closely associated with the deceased, and without knowledge of Dr. Craig's intentions, felt there was significance in the missing vial of insulin and came to me."

Ed gave them time to respond, but no one moved or changed expression.

"Since both Mr. Verian Riff's search of the Riff house and the one made by my office failed to produce the missing vial, we proceeded with the investigation along other lines. We asked all the medical men involved to give us educated guesses as to what actually happened while Adolf Riff was at home alone. They are in agreement that most probably Adolf had a mild seizure, returned to his bed until his heart beat returned to normal, and fell asleep, sleeping well past his usual lunch hour. Upon waking he made an effort to get food immediately, but either suffered another seizure, or his blood sugar dropped so dramatically that he went into coma, *or* a combination of these events. I think we can accept that as a reasonable assumption, don't you agree?"

Ed looked from one to the other.

"Seems logical," Verian said.

"I agree," Renata said.

"I suppose it does," Russell smiled inanely. "However, I can't see that that solves anything. We all knew it was something like that, only why?"

Russell was still playing games, Ed thought. He said, "There are several possibilities. Adolf's medication was very finely balanced. Had he received, for example, less than his normal dose of insulin and had his digitalis been increased in strength, say from his usual point-one-twenty-five milligrams to point-twenty-five, the change could well have been fatal."

"Then that's what happened," Russell said, "otherwise he would have been all right."

Russell looked from one to the other nodding, not actually saying, *I told you so.*

"To accomplish that," Ed said smoothly, "it would have been necessary to, say, substitute water for the insulin left in the vial Adolf used, which would have meant first extracting the insulin. To increase the digitalis would mean obtaining tablets of the stronger dosage from a pharmacy or some other source. Either procedure implies premeditation."

The room was completely quiet. Ed saw no movement other than Renata's eyes as her glance moved from Russell to Verian.

"We have checked," Ed continued, "and no local pharmacy has supplied any of you with point twenty-five milligram tablets of digitalis. If any of you obtained them it was most probably from some friend who uses tablets of that strength."

Verian's glance slid over to Russell's face.

"Tampering with the insulin vials would have required both time and know-how. I believe, Mr. Revolo, you can safely assume that Miss Riff did not alter her brother's medication, first because she had no ready source of higher strength digitalis tablets. Second, Adolf suffered no ill effects from use of the vial before the day in question. On that day, Miss Riff was never alone in the kitchen, therefore she had no opportunity to tamper with the insulin."

Russell looked at Verian, then at a spot behind Ed's head, and after an audible indrawn breath, said, "Are you suggesting that either Verian or I did?"

Ed smiled slightly. "If you will read the autopsy report handed you, Mr. Revolo, I am reasonably sure you can accept the county medical examiner's findings as proof of innocence for all of you. Adolf Riff died of natural causes as stated in the death certificate signed by the physician in attendance at the time of death."

Ed paused briefly, then added, "You may wish to pursue the theory of the altered medication further, in which case I suggest you engage a capable attorney."

The look Verian gave Russell lasted only a fleeting moment. It was a self-satisfied sneer. Russell's face was set in a pale, expressionless mask. Ed found the reactions of both men alarming.

9

Ed didn't pause to look back when they left the Riff house. Mike started the engine, pulled away from the curb and waited until he stopped Ed's unmarked vehicle at the intersection before he asked, "What do you think, Captain?"

"I think Verian warned Russell against this move and very likely challenged him to find a better way. I believe Russell will try again."

Mike drove slowly to the next boulevard stop. "Well, Captain," he said, "you put them all on notice. Renata should understand her situation and Verian certainly got the message. He knows we found his source of point-two-five dig. What do you think they did with the insulin vial?"

"It's probably back in the refrigerator along with the unused vials."

"This Russell," Mike shook his head. "I gotta agree, Captain, he played his long shot and lost. Next time he'll take a more direct approach. He'll have to hurry though. Bart Cameron means to marry the girl. He was in Spires Jewelry looking at rings."

"Maybe he'll take her on a long, long vacation," Ed said. "Or is that too much to hope for?"

Renata stood at the bay window watching the unmarked sheriff's car pull away. She was aware of movement behind her, but didn't turn until there was no more sound. She was surprised to see Verian sitting quietly in the club chair, the lamplight falling kindly on his sandy good looks.

"Come sit down, Renata." Verian motioned to a chair facing him.

She moved slowly, but did as he asked.

"The captain kind of laid it on the line tonight, and I guess I can understand that you'd like us all to clear out pronto. Can't blame you. I know there's nothing legally binding in Adolf giving me lifetime living privileges in my apartment and of course you can force me out."

"I've been thinking about it," Renata said.

"Well, you'll have to do it that way. I've got no place to go. I'm happy here with my own things and I like running the house."

Renata only shrugged. She had nothing to say. All she wanted now was a little time alone to sort things out before she called

Bart. She really wanted Bart. She thought she would like to cry on his shoulder. She was hurting deep inside. She *needed* Bart.

"You can believe what you will," Verian went on, "but I never did anything to harm Adolf. I didn't tinker with his medication, Renata. The dosages you gave him were exactly the amounts prescribed, I swear it. I've watched over Adolf, watched his diet, saw to it he followed Craig's orders, did everything for him I could. I loved him, and he loved me. You think it over, then if you want me out, you tell John Silas. He'll know what to do. 'Til then, I'll try to stay out of your way if that's what you want."

Renata turned a glance on Verian that bore the full force of her bitter anger. After a long moment she said, "I'll let you know. On your way to your rooms you can tell Russell to take his wife to a motel for the rest of the night and have the movers here for his things before noon tomorrow or he'll find them in the street."

To her surprise, Verian grinned. "Sure," he said. "Goodnight, Renata."

When Bart drove up, Renata ran out to meet him, but there had been no place for them to go. Bart had eaten dinner with his family, and Renata didn't want food. Until Russell was out of the Riff house, she didn't want to be there, so they had walked along the beach in front of the row of summer cottages. They strolled while she poured out her story, then when she began to cry, they stopped and he held her while she sobbed out her hurt and her fury. He kissed her and comforted her and held in his own anger. When she had quieted, they walked again, back the way they had come.

"I don't know, Bart," Renata said, "I was much too angry to be afraid. You see, I've known from the Sunday night the chandelier fell that they would try something, but this whole thing has been so outrageous, I really never felt threatened. However, after Ed Staple had me in his office and then when he had us all together, I could see what Russell was hoping for wasn't necessarily proof. All he needed was an official admission that foul play was a possibility. Given that, he would have produced the insulin vial with my fingerprints all over it, made a big thing about my intention to oust him (Adolf's protector) and a lot of other little things. Along with the altered medication theory, he might have made it work if Ed hadn't practically proved premeditation and access to the stronger digitalis dosage would be necessary."

"Are you convinced this was more than just seizing opportunity?" Bart asked.

"I don't know. I don't care for myself, but while I listened to Ed all I could think of was Adolf. He trusted those two. He loved them. He was never anything but good and kind and generous. They're monsters, both of them."

Bart stopped and held her close, feeling her

tremble; feeling tenderness for her override his anger.

"Maybe Staple is wrong. Maybe Verian is telling the truth and he didn't alter the medication. He did love Adolf, Renata."

"Uncle Verian is a gambler," Renata said. "My father gave him a home because he got in trouble for swindling a lady friend to pay his gambling debts. Dad strictly controlled the money he gave Uncle Verian, and I suppose Mother did the same. He has probably gone back to his old habits."

The trembling had stopped, although she stayed within the circle of his arms.

"Bart, they'll try again, you know. They want the Riff estate."

Bart took one arm from around her to lift her face, and with a crooked finger under her chin, he bent to kiss her.

"Do whatever you wish with the Riff estate, darling, but we're getting married and that will be the end of Mr. Revolo and Uncle Verian in your life."

"Verian has a point, Bart. Both Mother and Adolf gave him a lifetime living privilege in their wills. I'll have to talk to John Silas. For now, I don't think I'll bother."

"Okay, we'll cross that bridge after we're married."

She said nothing, but leaned against him for a moment, then she slipped one arm around his waist and they walked on.

"I feel almost human again, Bart. I was ready to come apart. It's so great having someone again. You never know how important that is until there's just you and your fears and you don't dare turn to the ones who might help. I'll always remember this night."

Bart stopped and hugged her close and kissed her. They were silent for a while, alone on the beach in the dim glow from the town lights. His cheek rested against her hair.

"Renata, I keep saying we're going to get married and you keep saying nothing. I *did* propose, and I thought you accepted. Didn't you?"

"Oh, yes, Bart. I want to marry you, you know that."

"Then let's set a date. Even then we'll have to have blood tests, get the license. There are things to do. It will take time."

"I know."

"Well, then . . ."

"There are things you have to know."

"If you mean those missing six years, forget them. If you think they'll cause a row, then wait until it's too late to back out."

Renata laughed. "If only it were that simple."

"Then tell me and get it over with."

"I suppose I must, but not here on the beach."

"Meanwhile, back to the original question. When, Renata?"

She pulled away from him and turned to watch the quiet surf. Marriage meant sex. She had shut that out of her mind. It would have to be faced. She couldn't go into marriage with all that buried in her past.

Would it change things? Would he want her? How would he react? Oh, dear Lord, could she do it—give her body? Would she panic? This was Bart. This was love. This was . . . This was terrifying.

Bart touched her cheek, turning her head to look up at him. "When, Renata?"

"Let me talk to John Silas first, then we'll decide."

"All right. Talk to John tomorrow, we'll settle things tomorrow night."

She smiled up at him, suddenly happy and free. "I'm sure Russell will be out of the house now. Let's go home, Bart."

He lifted her off her feet to kiss her, and then they were running along the sandy beach, back to the car. She stumbled. He caught her up, laughing, pulling her into his arms to carry her the last hundred feet. Her arms were around his neck, her head on his shoulder. It would be all right, everything would work out. Renata joined in the laughter.

Verian stood at the window in Renata's bedroom, being careful to keep far enough back so as not to be seen from the street below.

"She's gone," he said to Russell.

"For how long?"

"Long enough. She'll give you plenty of time to get out. She's in love."

"Do you think they'll marry?"

"If Bart has anything to do with it, as soon as possible. He's been in love with her since they were kids. So has she, only it took her longer to realize it. Augustin was stricter than most fathers, and they hadn't much chance as teenagers."

"Where was he when Augustin died and she needed him?"

"He took a job, he and his father both, with a big construction firm on a long term project in El Paso, Texas so Bart could go to college. With that raft of kids, he had to pay his own way."

"Very noble," Russell said. "Did you prepare dinner? I'm starved."

"Sure, but after Staple's little visit, I didn't mention it to Renata."

"Well, put it on the table while I go through things up here."

"Sure," Verian said. He watched Russell for a moment, refraining from saying a search of Renata's things would be useless. There was nothing to use against her, she was as pure as spring water.

They had finished dinner, and Audrey had gone to her room to pack. She had been angry and upset and silent.

"Find anything suggestive in Renata's things?" Verian asked.

Russell gave a derisive snort. "No. There was nothing in her duffel bag but a couple of towels and sheets. She has no clothes. Jeans and a few shirts and that awful nylon jacket.

She has bought a couple of pretty nice dresses, but that's it, except for the skirt and sweater she's wearing. There's not even a scrap of paper in that room."

Verian toyed with his coffee cup and didn't say any of the things he was thinking.

"I'm going to miss all this like hell," Russell said.

"You know what has to be done before you can get back in."

"It's pretty short notice. Why didn't you persuade her to let the Sunday deadline stand?"

"I'm not sure how long I can hang on myself, going to bat for you would have been the end."

"Do you think she'll let you stay? You've got to. We've got to have you in the house."

"What for? I told you, there's no way I'm going to push her down the stairs, and let me tell you, she sure as hell won't fall."

Russell left the table and came back with a bottle of brandy and two glasses.

"Nothing for me," Verian said.

Russell held the cut glass tumbler up to the light and sighed. Cut glass like this would cost him a fortune. He sipped the brandy, swirled it in the glass and stared at nothing. Verian patiently waiting.

"Okay," Russell said, and drained the glass. "I've got it worked out, but you'll have to help, and we'll need to think about timing. Not too soon, but we can't give Bart Cameron time to talk her into marrying him. Come on,

I'll show you what I have in mind. We'll have some rigging to do."

Verian pushed back his chair. "This had better work, Russell, it's the only chance we're likely to get. And make it fast, you haven't much time left."

10

From her bedroom window, Renata looked down over the quiet night time street. She was feeling restless. Her nerves were raw. A car turned at the intersection and Renata stepped back out of the line of sight. It was Verian coming home.

There had been a row with John Silas over Verian, and Bart had sided with the attorney. Her decision to let Verian stay had been based largely on her fear that she would be forced to run again. If she did, Verian might as well live here, it would be better than leaving the house empty. Russell she had been adamant about. If he set foot on the place he was to be arrested. Silas had his instructions.

She was having a will drawn up with Bart the principal heir. Adolf had taken care of

Verian. Adolf had been surprisingly wise, she thought. Sixty percent of the cash had gone to Russell, with all the income property held in trust for Verian with John Silas as executor. At Verian's death the estate would be divided among the younger Reveras who were Adolf's favorite cousins.

Renata had been to see George Kettleman. She could trust George. Anywhere she went, she would be financially secure, that was all set up. The next step was to get a passport and visa, whatever she might need for foreign travel, she couldn't afford to leave any possible avenue of escape unexplored. She wondered if it might be wise to have an airline ticket ready with an open date. It wouldn't matter where, just to some large city with multiple choices for further travel.

Perhaps it would be a good idea to tell Bart she would like a European honeymoon—say to Spain. They could both get passports, then it would look normal. How long would that take? A week? Two? That could be their wedding day, the day the passports were validated. With luck, it might be possible, they might make it. Did she dare take the chance?

Renata left her room and went into the back bedroom that had a window overlooking the back yard and Verian's private entrance into his wing of the house. She watched until the light went out, but didn't move away immediately.

Thoughts of Adolf, dead at not quite thirty, preoccupied her. Had Verian manipulated the medication and thereby shortened his life? If so, by how much? Couldn't he have waited? How desperate was he? Surely Adolf would have paid any reasonable debt. Well, Verian had enough income now. But then, how much was enough? There was all that property her father had accumulated for so little that was now worth so much, and she stood in the way. After her there was only Verian. He must have counted on it being his before she had come home. She could understand the temptation—she had had her own.

What would he do now? What would *they* do? She mustn't forget Russell. Russell was the motivating force. It was really Russell she had to fear. Russell . . . and Tanner.

Renata returned to her room and watched the street again for a few moments before she went to bed. It was ten minutes to twelve. She had dropped off to sleep when a small foreign car pulled up to the curb opposite the Riff house and stopped briefly. The driver let down the window and looked up at the front bedroom on the third floor, then drove on. She was there. That was enough. There were certain arrangements to be made. Another day or two, then he would be ready.

"You've got to be kidding, Renata," Bart said. "You're not only letting him stay, nothing has changed. You're letting him continue to run the house, do the cooking. He's going on as if nothing has happened."

"Why not? Verian is a chef, a real one. He's

doing a beef roast and I asked him to make Yorkshire pudding."

"Renata . . . !"

"I know, he would like to see me dead, and he probably shortened Adolf's life. He's still a superb cook. He's here. We're here. He should do something to earn his keep, so let's enjoy a good meal while we can." She kissed Bart. "Come on, we'll have a drink before dinner."

Bart stood in the center of the living room, feet planted solidly, his whole body a rock of resistance, his face set in uncharacteristically rigid, stubborn lines.

"He shouldn't be here."

"Of course he shouldn't. He should have the grace to leave, but he hasn't, so we'll make use of his talents. He won't join us for the social hour."

Bart stood where he was, looking down at her, his expression unchanged.

"All right," Renata shrugged. "Where shall we go? Or can we decide that while we have our drink? You can pour . . . or is it mix? I'll have white wine and there's all kinds of booze and mixes."

Bart let out a held breath and went to the bar. He could use a good stiff shot of bourbon. He handed Renata her wine and sat beside her on the sofa.

"You realize it's almost Christmas."

"Yes. We ought to talk about it. Verian asked if I wanted a tree."

"Verian . . ." Bart said and stopped. He

reached into his jacket pocket and brought out a small, blue box. "Somehow things never quite work out as I plan them. I wanted giving you this to be something special and romantic, but right now I feel the important thing is to get it on your finger, then maybe I'll begin to believe I'll actually get you in front of a preacher."

Renata took the blue box, held it a moment while she looked into blue eyes that were again gentle and loving. She opened the box and gave a little gasp of pleasure. The ring was a diamond surrounded with small sapphires. She gave it back to him as she extended the third finger of her left hand.

"It's perfect," she said. "I love you, Bart."

They were in each other's arms, the world forgotten, when Verian said, "Sorry to break up this love scene, but you've got plenty of time and Yorkshire pudding is best while it's hot."

As they broke off the kiss, Renata looked at Bart and gave a little shrug as she turned toward Verian.

"Oh, what the hell," Bart said. "Let's eat."

"About Christmas," Renata said when they had returned to the living room with their after dinner coffee, "why don't we give ourselves a fabulous honeymoon? Let's go to Spain, and maybe from there we'll cruise the Mediterranean."

He took her left hand, holding it up to look

at the ring. "It suits you," he said. "I knew it would."

"You suit me."

"About the honeymoon, I had something a little less fabulous in mind, like maybe a week in Hawaii."

"I'd really like the European trip, Bart. I'd like some time and a lot of distance between me and all this."

He toyed with the ring. "I've got a job, honey."

"I know. Would three weeks be impossible?"

"Just about."

"Two?"

"Well, maybe."

"We'll have to get passports. We'll get married the day they're valid and be ready to leave on the first plane out. Okay?"

"Okay. We'll work on it."

"Then it's settled."

"It's settled," Bart said, and took her into his arms.

Verian, standing in the entry, turned and went into his own apartment, closing and locking the connection door behind him. He went to his private telephone and dialed.

"Russell, you'd better plan to make your move," Verian said, and told Russell what he had overheard.

Ed took his grey flannel jacket from the formed wooden hanger, and returned the hanger to the coat rack in the corner of his office. He put on the jacket, moving his shoulders to settle it into place. He was wearing the predominantly red paisley corduroy vest today. Today he was going to see the sheriff about the Riff case. He wasn't worried about it, just irritated.

It was Friday afternoon, so he left the office early to drive into the county seat. The Riff case should have been marked closed and filed. He wanted the sheriff to know from him that he had departed from strict departmental policy in handling the matter of Adolf's death, and that he suspected Renata's reasons for coming to him in the beginning were well founded.

Ed spent the better part of an hour with the sheriff, going over facts and theory, hoping for something he didn't get. He came away realizing the truth of Renata's original statement: there was nothing anyone could do *before* the fact.

In Adolf's case, there was nothing he could do after the fact. Ed was totally convinced Verian had altered Adolf's medication over a period of six months. He was therefore guilty of murder regardless of the undeniable fact that, at best, Adolf had only a short time to live. It rankled that Verian was untouchable.

Before he left the county seat, Ed called Jamie and asked her to have dinner with him. When she agreed, he called the Santa Barbara Biltmore for reservations, then drove to the Cold Creek Trout Farm. He would be early, in time to help with the evening chores, and afterward, while he waited for Jamie to dress, he would have time to spend with her collection of duck decoys. Each time he went, he found one he had missed before. There were several from Mason's Decoy Factory he wanted to examine. Should he find one for sale, Ed wanted to know it was authentic.

They had cocktails in the big, pleasant room at the Biltmore facing the ocean, sitting in comfortable over-stuffed chairs.

"I'm glad you did this, Ed," Jamie said. "I needed a bit of elegance in my life. I do sometimes feel inundated with fish."

"You could sell out."

She laughed, pleasantly. "Then what would I do? Work in some office? No thanks. I like it —the fish farm. It's called aquafarming these days and is beginning to be big business, although of course, not my style."

"You could sell off the decoys and live comfortably by investing your capital."

"Poor Ed," Jamie smiled as she sipped her drink. "I sometimes wonder if you'll ever call again. Seeing them must be torture."

"Seeing them is a privilege I appreciate, but the ducks aren't what keep me coming back to that stone house. It's you. Every time I get up tight about something, I find myself thinking of you."

Jamie gave him a keen glance, then looked away.

"What has you up tight tonight?" she asked.

"That didn't come off right, did it?" Ed smiled. "It's the Riff case. I came to tell the sheriff about it. We were asked to look into the Adolf Riff death. If it hadn't been that Renata had come to see us, we might have sent it to the district attorney."

Ed finished his drink and signaled for another. Jamie refused. "Thing is," he went on, "I'm afraid this is only phase one. I'm afraid Renata made some shrewd guesses of a general, if not a specific nature, and I have played into her hands."

Ed twirled the ice in his empty glass, and shrugged. "Taking criticism from the boss doesn't bother me, but I have this growing conviction that Renata is by no means through with me and my office."

"You mean you've been had on the carpet by the sheriff?"

"Well, sort of. We agree by handling it through our office we probably saved everyone concerned some unpleasant publicity."

"So it's all right."

"Sure. There's a clear and present danger to Renata. I can justify my position. Question is, how wise have I been? It isn't just the Verian and Russell thing, there's an undercurrent that is almost palpable. I can't shake the feeling that she's manipulating everyone."

His drink came. Ed smiled at Jamie and

lifted his glass. "I wonder what you would think of her."

"She sounds like quite a woman."

"She's a tiny person, but there's breeding and amazing vitality. There's a fierce look that comes into her eyes, almost hawklike, except that she's more the hunted than the hunter."

"Self-protection," Jamie said. "Perhaps she's had to be."

Ed laughed. "Perhaps that's it."

He looked at Jamie and smiled and began to feel contented. "Forget Renata," he said. "That's why I wanted to be with you. I'd like to close the Riff case. I've been wondering if maybe I want to forget the job altogether."

She looked up at him in surprise. "You mean quit—resign?"

"Or move on, maybe back to a city job. My health is good. The swimming keeps me fit. I could pass any physical tests now. I may not be able to further down the road. There's still the bullet near the spine they couldn't remove. It's something to think about."

The cocktail waitress told them quietly that their table was ready, and picking up their half-finished drinks, led them into the dining room.

While Jamie studied the menu, Ed studied Jamie. Pastel coloring, but more than just pretty. Beautiful? Well—Elegant? Maybe classic was closer. What was her blood line, he wondered. Nordic? No. Irish? Saxon?

Renata's blondness was different. In spite of her fair hair and blue eyes, the volatile Latin temperament was there.

There was something deeper in both women. Something at once different and the same. A female pride, perhaps. They were, Ed thought, each in her own way, aristocrats. The concept intrigued him, whether or not it was true.

Jamie was buttering bread when she paused and looked up at Ed. There was no particular expression in her eyes when he met her glance.

"I'm surprised you would ever consider giving up your place in Port Haven. You seem so 'of a piece,' so integrated with the job, if you strip away all the present social connotations attached to that word. Why, I wonder? And I wonder if you know. Do you?"

Ed laughed. "You have asked the sixty-four thousand dollar question. I feel I'm marking time. I'm bored and that scares me." He watched her long, slender hands as she buttered the bread, not daring to look into her face. "The real trouble may be I'm afraid I'm falling in love."

Her hands stopped moving. He looked up from them to meet her startled glance.

"Me?"

He nodded.

"Oh, Ed. Don't."

Renata piled up her pillows and scrooched up in bed so she could see the predawn sky through the window. After a while she went to the window and looked out over the town to the dark waters of the Pacific. Renata twisted the ring on her finger. What was she thinking of? How could she do what she had done? Even if there was time for a wedding—time even for a honeymoon—there could only be one end. The end was Tanner—always Tanner.

She had gone this far, she would go the rest of the way. She would know this little respite of happiness, it could never be taken from her. With the estate, she would never need to worry over money, that much she could be grateful for, although she would trade it all for Bart—just Bart.

The sky had become opaque. Trees and buildings had sharply outlined silhouettes. Renata turned her gaze from the window. A walk on the beach, she thought, alone to think things through, check to be sure she had taken care of everything possible, that she was ready to run.

She was dressed and out of the house in fifteen minutes, and on the beach before it was full daylight. The sun was over the ridge of mountain when she decided to have breakfast in the waterfront cafe where she had first talked with Bart.

The coffee was hot and warming after the long walk in the cool, damp air of the morning. She loved the smell of the sea, but the coffee smell was equally good and stirred memories of mornings aboard *The Alva* when her father took her fishing. The bacon and eggs came, her cup was refilled, she buttered toast and spread jam, not thinking, just being, absorbed in her food.

Men came in and were greeted. There was talk at the counter stools. She didn't look up. The door opened. There was a fractional pause that said *stranger*.. It was *him*. She didn't have to see, she knew. She took a bite of egg, and a bite of toast, and he was sliding into the booth opposite her.

"Hello, sweetheart."

She looked up, staring steadily into the perpetually youthful face framed with the "darling" brown curls. Tanner's eyes were light brown. The left lid drooped at the outer corner. The vision in the left eye had been impaired. That had been her doing. The eye had a tick, a nerve jerked constantly. It must be annoying, she thought, as she continued to chew her food.

When she had swallowed and taken a sip of coffee, she said, "Hello, Tanner."

He smiled. A turning up of the corners of his mouth. "Very foolish of you, coming home."

She didn't reply.

"You're on my turf, you know."

"Mine too," Renata said.

He laughed, high pitched. An ugly sound.

"Since you're here, sweetheart, I have made plans. Disfiguring you won't be enough. We'll take up where we left off, only

124

this time there will be no escape—ever. I'm sure you understand me."

She didn't answer, but put down her fork. Another bite would be impossible.

"Go ahead and eat, sweetheart. I don't have much more to tell you, just that Bart Cameron will take Alva's and Adolf's place. Marry him, he's a dead man." Tanner's lips turned up at the corners. "Really, I don't know why I'm so good to you, warning you all the time. I must like to see you squirm, but this time there'll be no cat and mouse game, Renata my sweet. This time it's for real."

He stood, a little man, only a few inches taller than she. He gave his high pitched, ugly laugh, picked up her check, and said, "I'll take care of this for you. Eat hearty, sweetheart, and remember about Bart, won't you? Such a nice young man to die so soon."

11

It was a full minute after Tanner disappeared before Renata moved—before she felt she could breathe. He hadn't changed his style of dress, she noticed, but still wore the tailor-made cowboy clothes with the welted yokes and the flat felled seams and the boots with heels. He thought the lines gave him height and breadth of shoulder, whereas they made him look ridiculous and called attention to his size.

Renata reached into her jacket pocket for tip money. She needed to get away before the trembling began as it usually did after one of Tanner's sudden appearances. Seeing him always brought it all back and terror would seize her. She felt surprised that it hadn't already begun. Tanner often waited for it. He would come upon her in some place that gave him maneuverability: a busy street, a parking lot, a church. Any place where he could deliver his message and disappear into a crowd.

The first time had been the worst. She was in a crosswalk when that voice had said, "Hello, Renata, sweetheart." She had almost fainted and he had helped her across the street. Terror had totally possessed her, and she had run, leaving her job with a small printing firm, taking a bus out of town, only to see him pass in his red Corvette and wave. She had left the bus in a crossroads community and hitchhiked in the opposite direction, leaving her traveling case behind, carrying only her handbag with a few dollars she had saved.

She had survived and he had found her. Always he found her. Once she had refused to run, and that time he threw the acid. She had the scar on her shoulder as a reminder that he meant to disfigure and mutilate her as he promised. She had been lucky, but she never again tested her luck. She had run—and run —and run again.

This would be the last time. Even if she was forced to run to save Bart, this would be the last. She had no doubt he meant what he said. If she married, he would have Bart killed. It would give him pleasure. Just as it had pleased him to torment Alva. The threats of disfigurement and lingering death against both Alva and Adolf had been real.

Alva had been pitiable after the demonstration. A man, a huge man, by Alva's description, had opened the car door and poured out the contents of a small bottle on the passenger seat. In seconds the acid had eaten its way through the upholstery. The huge man had grinned broadly and shaken the few remaining drops into Alva's lap. After that, Renata had left home for good. She couldn't endanger her mother and Adolf.

The waitress poured coffee into Renata's cup. "Was something wrong?" she asked. "You hardly touched your breakfast." Renata looked up, said everything was fine, she just wasn't hungry after all. The waitress moved away, still Renata didn't leave, but sat holding the tip change in her hand.

How long had he been in Port Haven? Long enough to know about Bart. Long enough to cover every possible avenue of escape. Renata looked through the cafe window and watched a trawler moving along the channel, putting out to sea. Well, maybe not every avenue. It had worked once, why not again? The fishing boats. Tanner had no control over the fishermen, and most of them would remember her father.

At two o'clock on Saturday evening, Ed called Suzanna from Santa Barbara where he was doing some Christmas shopping to check for messages and say he wouldn't be home until later.

"That Detective Mike Wiley called about an hour ago," Suzanna said. "He thought you'd like to know Bart Cameron gave Renata a diamond and sapphire ring and they are going to Spain on their honeymoon."

"Can't happen too soon," Ed said. "Anything else?"

"You buying a ring on this shopping trip?"

"No, not this time," Ed said lightly. "Did Mike have any other news?"

"Just that the Revolos don't live there any more, and it looks like the case that came in on Wednesday is closed. They got a confession."

"Okay, thanks, Suzanna. Have a nice weekend."

Ed had made his call from the La Cumbre Shopping Center, and on his way to the pay phone, he had passed Slavick's Jewelers. Not a ring for Jamie, but perhaps a necklace, or one of those slender chains with a pendant, a small stone, but perfect. Ed retraced his steps and stood looking at the window display.

So Cameron had given Renata diamonds and sapphires. Probably suited her. Ed took a moment to wish them happiness and an extended stay in Spain. The marriage should end all danger to her, since it would put another person between Verian and the Riff fortune. Ed looked at the window but no longer saw the display. If marriage ended the threat to Renata's life, it also shortened the time Russell and Verian had to take it from her. Where was she, Ed wondered? What kind of precautions was she taking, if any?

Surely she realized the pressure time put on the two men, didn't she? Damn! Should he put a tail on both of them? He'd better. Ed went back to the phone. The assignment made, he had done what he could.

Ed strolled leisurely, window shopping as he went, and paused again in front of Slavick's Jewelers. He couldn't overdo it, that would be fatal. He let his thoughts run over the scene in the Biltmore. She had said, "Oh, Ed. Don't," in such a strange, haunted way he had wondered, and then it had come out.

"All right," he had said, smiling at her. "Don't panic. You're doubtless right. I shouldn't fall in love. Few women want to marry a man in my profession."

"It isn't your profession," she had said.

"It's me then."

"No, of course not. I like you. I like your mind, your modus operandi, and I enjoy being with you. Can't that be enough?"

"Who could ask for more?" He had grinned at her. "I feel the same way, only lately I've been wondering why. Falling in love scares the hell out of me. I did that once."

"You told me. Her name was Marie Elena, wasn't it?"

"Yes. So don't panic, okay, and decide not to see me any more."

She didn't respond right away. Finally she said, "I don't think I could handle love. Not that kind. I'd be afraid there would be children and then it would go sour. I like our relationship the way it is, Ed.''

"Then we'll keep it that way."

He knew that, when she was a very vulnerable thirteen, her parent's divorce had resulted in a bitter court battle, and that her mother had remarried more than once. He had changed the subject to trout farming and they had worked their way back into their usual easy camaraderie. Give her time, he had thought, and wondered which of them needed it more.

Ed went inside Slavick's, selected an older male salesperson, and told him what he wanted. He came out with a teardrop shaped sapphire gemstone suspended from a slender platinum chain. He hoped Jamie would love it as he was sure Renata loved her ring. Ed felt tempted to drive up the mountain and give it to her now, without waiting for Christmas. Instead, he ate lobster at The Lobster House on Cabrillo Boulevard.

Saturday evening. If he wanted a date he should have made arrangements before dinner. Ed shrugged. Not tonight.

At home, after he had done his prescribed forty laps in the pool, he lit a fire in his living room, and settled down to a quiet evening alone. He read a while, called the station. There was nothing on either Verian or Russell so he went to bed.

It was eleven when Ed turned out the lights. He wondered, should he check the Riff house himself? No, Bart would take care of Renata. His last waking thought was to wonder if Jamie would enjoy a weekend in the Coachella Valley.

Verian answered the phone in the alcove, and Russell said, "Can you talk?"

"No." Verian spat out the word. "She's here. It's four o'clock on Saturday, what did you expect? You're lucky she didn't answer."

"Then go to your apartment. I'll call you there."

Verian looked into the living room. It was unoccupied. Renata hadn't come down yet, and a good thing. He stood in the entry and looked up the stairwell, listening. Presently, he heard a door open and then another close. After a minute, Verian could hear water running. He nodded, satisfied, and went into his apartment, closing and locking the connecting door. The phone was ringing.

"Okay," Verian said when he lifted the receiver. "She's in the shower, you can talk."

"Two things," Russell said. "First, she's making a new will."

"How do you know?"

"I know. That's enough."

"What's in it?"

"Basically, Bart Cameron gets all the Riff land and most of the money. Things held jointly with the Riveras go to them. You get the house."

Verian grunted. "Damn decent of her."

"Well, considering the circumstances,"

Russell said. "This is a rough draft of the will, it isn't ready for signing. She still has to approve everything. Monday or Tuesday, I'd say."

"Doesn't leave much time."

"That's only half of it."

When Russell didn't go on, Verian said impatiently, "Well, drop the other shoe."

"Staple has put a tail on me. In a town this size it's easy to spot. You probably have one. When you hang up, take a careful look out the front window."

"Okay. I suppose we'd better call the whole thing off."

"No," Russell's voice was sharp. "We use this to our advantage. Now listen." His voice became persuasive, "You're going to have to take a more active part."

"Forget it. No way."

"Just listen," Russell's voice carried calm authority.

Verian listened, not commenting. When Russell was through, he said, "We'll take them one, two, three. Number one, no, too risky in the time I have. Number two, okay, I can do that. Number three, if I have a chance, otherwise I'll leave the dead batteries in my apartment where you can see them. That's the best I can do."

"It's enough," Russell said. "Call me back and let me know what's happening."

"Russell," Verian said, "you're sure about that will?"

"Positive."

Verian said nothing.

"All right," Russell said, "I'm sitting in Silas's office with the document in my hand. There's an appointment on the desk calendar: Riff will, Monday at eleven."

"I get the house. That's it?"

"For your lifetime, then it goes to Cameron."

"Cameron," Verian repeated. "Not one of the Riveras? To Cameron?"

"That's right. The rough draft is ready and seems complete, although it's complicated."

"I wouldn't have minded the Riveras too much," Verian's voice sounded sad, "Consuella—that bunch. But Cameron." Verian chewed his bottom lip and thought. "Okay, Russell, better me than him," he said, and quietly replaced the receiver.

12

Renata paced the living room floor. In the hours since Tanner's appearance she had put into motion the plans half formed in the month she had been at home. So much depended on the actions of others it had been impossible to do more than think in generalities. Now that Tanner was here, her thoughts had definite shape, although nothing was final. She had taken care of the legal things, but there were people to see, arrangements to make—vital arrangements.

Renata sat and stared out the front window. She paced. She sat. She was waiting for Bart. When he came it was with a buoyant happiness. He lifted her from the floor and swung her around.

"I've got the passport pictures, and I checked with the travel agent. In this county you get passport applications at the county courthouse, but we can go to the Federal Building in Los Angeles and save the mailing time. For a fee, they will send the passports directly to us within five working days. I've made arrangements to go on Monday. What do you think of that, me darlin'?"

She smiled, and laughed, and did her best to match his enthusiasm. He put her down as Verian came in with a tray of hors d'oeuvres.

"Thought you'd like a bit of a snack with your drinks," he said as he placed the tray on a coffee table. "Are you going out, or shall I whip up something for you? I got some nice steaks on special. Dinner in half an hour."

"Okay, that's very nice of you, Verian," Bart said, and after Verian had returned to the kitchen, he added, "I guess he's trying to make amends. Maybe you were right in letting him stay."

"Don't be snowed," Renata said. "The decision was expedient that's all. Fix the drinks, and I'll have one this time, but we'll take them into the library where we can shut the door. This is story telling time, Bart."

Like rooms of its period, the library was lined with bookshelves and paneling. It had a large flattop desk and big comfortable chairs with a love seat on one side of the fireplace. She put the hors d'oeuvre tray on the butler's tray in front of the love seat and went to close the door behind Bart, who was carrying the drinks.

Renata went to the front window, being

careful to keep out of the direct light, but giving herself a view of the street. She kept still for long enough to get her thoughts in order. For his own protection she must tell Bart about Tanner, but how much was enough to convince him of the danger? The whole sordid tale, she supposed. With a sigh of resignation, she turned and went and sat beside him on the love seat.

"I want to marry you, Bart. I have never wanted anything so completely, but there are things you must know first, then if you just walk out, I'll understand."

He handed her her drink, then settled back, smiling. "Go ahead, darling, let's hear it and get it behind us. I'll tell you now, I'm not walking."

Renata took a sip of the drink. He had made it too strong, but maybe it would help.

"You remember Tanner Grimes, don't you?"

Bart shrugged. "Maybe. A little guy. He went fishing once in a while. Is that the one?"

"Yes."

"A friend of your mother's wasn't he?"

"Her family and his have been friends for years. His older sister and my mother were about the same age, but there was no one near Tanner. Most of his friends were schoolmates from some boarding school in Los Angeles, I think. He ran with a different crowd, and he got into business very young. At least, that was what I thought those years when he fished with us."

Renata paused, her glance going once again to the front window. *I won't close the drapes,* she told herself. *I won't give him the satisfaction.* She drew in a deep breath and turned back to Bart.

"I never liked Tanner particularly. I thought he was cocky and a braggart, but he came to see us after father's death and was very thoughtful of me. I thought he had loved my father and that was all that counted with me at the time. You had gone to work for your uncle that summer. I was planning to go to college, but Dad's death had taken the fun out of everything. And then Mother married Alban."

Even today she couldn't keep down the sudden welling-up of hurt and anger, and paused to give the emotions time to drain away before she went on. During the pause, Bart took her hand.

"Look, honey, I don't care about Tanner or those lost six years, just so we don't lose any more. You're getting all worked up and upset. Forget it."

"Wouldn't that be wonderful. If only I could." She squeezed his hand and leaned over to kiss him lightly. "You must know, Bart."

Renata settled back, still holding Bart's hand, her head against the back of the sofa, her eyes half closed.

"Mother had sold *The Alva* and there were some things on board that belonged to Tanner. The next owner brought them here and Mother notified Tanner, asking him to pick them up. I'd been crying when he came, and I told him how I felt about Alban. He was sympathetic and understanding, and asked Mother if he could take me out to dinner. I didn't see him again for a while. The next time I was with a bunch of kids and we were pretty rowdy. I really went wild, Bart. I did all sorts of things, drinking, fast driving, even a little marijuana and some pretty heavy love making, but I never went to bed with any of them. Somehow before I got that far, Dad's face would float between me and the guy, and I'd hear him say, 'Don't sell yourself cheap, baby. You don't have to, you've got it all,' and somehow I'd wiggle out of it. That's what I was doing that night when I saw Tanner. Wiggling out. And I asked him to take me home."

A car passed by the street, and Renata went rigid until the sound diminished to nothing. She clung to Bart's hand even after she relaxed.

"I went out with Tanner a couple of times. We had a date the night of my big blow-up with Mother and Alban. I had come home to find Alban's portrait hanging in the living room in place of Dad's. They had even used the same frame. It was the final straw. They had been systematically getting rid of every reminder of my father, and when she refused to let me hang Dad's portrait in my own room, I just went berserk."

Bart withdrew his hand from hers in order

to slip his arm around her and pull her to him.

"Honey," he began at the moment a car drove slowly past. Renata jumped up and looked outside. It was Tanner. She knew what he would do: drive along the street every few minutes as long as Bart's truck was there. She must make Bart see the danger.

Seated beside him once more, Renata said, "Tanner was especially nice to me that night. I even liked him, and I let him make love to me a little."

She pulled away from him, and briefly covered her face with her hands.

"Renata," Bart said, but she stopped him with a look.

"Things got steadily worse at home. I got wilder, but I knew I was going to be forced to leave home. I just couldn't take Alban sitting in Dad's chair at the table and in the living room and watching my mother fawn and simper over him as if she were a teenager and he was some movie idol. I told Tanner, and, about the third time, he said if I meant it about leaving home, maybe he could help me. He asked me a lot of questions about what I thought I could do to make a living, and I said I didn't care, all I wanted was to get away."

Renata laughed bitterly. "Maybe Tanner was right and I did mislead him. He told me he had this house up in the Montecito Hills on an old estate, and he had a couple of girls there who worked for him. He said he was sure he could work things out, and the girls would be glad to show me the ropes."

Her laugh was almost a sob. "All I knew was that Tanner had a number of business interests, and seemingly lots of money. I don't know what I thought the job would be. I wasn't thinking, I was just emoting all over the place like some lovesick heroine in those old silent movies, but whatever I thought, I wasn't prepared to become a prostitute, no matter how glamorous the surroundings or how wealthy the perverts Tanner brought to his mansion."

"Prostitute!" Bart breathed the word in hushed tones.

Renata looked at his startled, incredulous expression and laughed. "Well, maybe they were more like call girls. There may be some kind of distinction. Anyway the house was a mansion behind a wall with iron gates set way back in a canyon. It was in the middle of several acres, very secluded. The girls were as gorgeous as the setting. Tanner said their job, and mine, would be to entertain important clients of his."

Renata looked up at the ceiling and blew air in that direction. "I don't see how I could have been so blind and so stupid, but it actually took me the better part of a week to really get the picture. Tanner kept me with him, took me to Los Angeles shopping for the right kind of clothes, filled me full of his supreme confidence in my ability to do the job for him. Then came the night when there was this important client, very difficult to please, but if I made him happy I could count on a big bonus. Tanner was briefing me on what this man expected when it hit me. I saw the whole picture in a flash. I was . . ."

The ringing of the telephone caused them both to jump. Renata let it ring five times, then went to the phone alcove and picked up the receiver after the sixth ring.

Tanner's voice said, "Renata, sweetheart, I warned you. If you care anything at all for Bart Cameron, send him home, and don't see him again."

Renata breathed into the receiver several times, then said, "Tanner, go to hell."

The line went dead on the sound of Tanner's high pitched, indecent laughter. Renata stood looking at the ornate French telephone that had been Alva's delight, until Bart called to her.

"What did he say, Renata?"

She repeated Tanner's words.

"He means it, Bart. He'll have you killed without fear for himself. He would enjoy it. You can't just shrug off Tanner, he's vicious and cruel and completely without conscience. He wants revenge, and now that he's caught me on home territory, he means to have it. I'll have to run again."

She stood beside the love seat, and he pulled her down beside him, to take her in his arms. She returned the kiss, letting it last, delaying the inevitable.

"I don't understand," Bart said at last. "Revenge for what?"

"For what I did to him. Once I realized what the set-up was, I was having no part of it. We had a terrible row. There was a moment when I thought he was going to let me go, but then he found out I was a virgin. At first he wouldn't believe it, then he got all excited. He'd never had a virgin and he decided to keep me for himself."

"He raped you?"

Renata gave a brief, bitter laugh. "Of course. He had to get me high on drugs to do the job. I fought him until he called for help. I don't remember much of the rest of the evening. The next day he was very pleased. He even talked about marriage. Two old California families. My size suited him. We were perfect for each other, he said. He was sorry about the way it happened, but we could forget that. We would have a Mexican wedding and a long, beautiful honeymoon."

Renata pulled away from Bart and turned to look at him. He was, she thought, too stunned to say anything. He looked at her as though he didn't comprehend what she was telling him. Well, he had to know, not only for his own protection, but because it was the only way there could ever be anything like trust between them . . . if by some miracle they had a chance at the future.

"When I refused Tanner's kind offer of marriage, he told me it was my only way out. There was no way he could turn me loose to blow the whistle on his very lucrative operation. I had three choices. Marry him, become a willing part of the establishment, or be a reluctant one—for as long as I was useful."

Bart said, "Now listen, Renata, there is no reason why you should run from this creep. You can be protected. He's a pimp and deals in drugs—"

Renata's laugh held scorn. "And I can't touch him. I tried. Mother tried when I got away and came home. We sent the police to his fabulous estate, and that's just what it was, a fabulous estate. The occupant wasn't even at home. He was in the hospital where I put him."

They sat in silence, looking at each other. Bart was thinking it through, seeing how Tanner would work things out. When he had circled around to the present, his lips set in a firm line and the usually gentle blue eyes glinted with determination.

"All right," Bart said, "let's hear the rest of it."

"Tanner kept me locked in my room, and at night he would have his goon help him give me drugs. I think it was the third day, but I'm not sure, when Tanner came in to tell me he would be gone for a couple of days."

Renata turned her head and looked at a spot on the wall above the fireplace. Her voice was low, husky with emotion. "While Tanner was gone the goon came into my room." She began to tremble.

"Don't go on, Renata, I get the picture only too well."

Bart took her into his arms and held her, but the trembling continued.

"He was a huge man," she said, "and when he was through, I knew I was in pretty bad shape. I was still bleeding when Tanner came home. He saw at once I would need a doctor, and he called one. He got rid of the goon, and sent the girls somewhere. I was supposed to say my assailant had broken into the house, raped me and fled. That's what he later told the police. There were only Tanner and myself in the house—or in the rooms we occupied. It was my only chance. The only weapon in the room was a chain on a hanging lamp. While Tanner was gone, I pulled it from the lamp, and when he came back into the room I beat him with it."

The trembling was more violent than ever. Bart held her close, smoothing her hair, saying softly, "Don't. Don't. Don't say any more. Don't relive it." But once started, she was unable to stop.

"I don't really know what I did. I just swung the thing and kept on swinging it until Tanner lay senseless on the floor, blood all over him, then I ran. I took his car. I knew where he kept the extra keys, and I knew the gate would be open for the doctor. I drove home and I told Mother and Alban what had happened. It was only later that I knew about Tanner. I had battered his face so he needed a lot of corrective surgery, and his left eye will never be right. But worse, he'll never really be a man again."

After a while the trembling stopped, and Renata pulled away from Bart.

"That's what Tanner wants revenge for, his manhood. That's why he has followed me, waiting for some moment like this." Renata took his hand in hers. "Bart, I can't stay here. My only chance is to get away—to run."

Bart murmured words of comfort, then fell silent for a while.

"I wasn't so far away that summer that I didn't hear things," he said at last. "I knew you were running with a wild crowd. I wanted to come home, but the job was six days a week and I needed every dollar for college. Then I heard you were in some kind of sanitarium and I thought there had probably been a pregnancy and an abortion. I knew that sort of thing would completely throw you, so I wasn't too surprised to learn that you had left home. That's the kind of confession I expected to hear. I didn't expect anything like this."

He was silent again, holding her, his face on her hair. "We'll work this out. We'll get married right away and I'll deal with Mr. Tanner Grimes."

The grimness in his voice brought her to her feet. She stood facing him, looking down at him, the terror she felt a pallid taste in her mouth. "No! Don't even think about it."

Renata paced the floor and returned to stand in front of Bart. "You've got to understand, Bart. You've got to believe Tanner is capable of doing exactly what he says. He's a little king with absolute power over his own people. He will have you killed and no one will ever suspect him. It will most likely be a perfectly believable accident no one will even think to question. He won't want to attract attention, he'll just kill you. He does have that power, Bart."

She paced the floor again. "Why did I get you into this? Why didn't I just take the inheritance and go? I knew he would find me. How well I knew it. Bart, I'm sorry. I love you so, and I just wanted to be normal and happy, I let myself believe I could make it work."

She stood looking down at him, feeling her misery, her fear, and realizing fully the danger in which Bart walked because of her.

There was a rap on the door, and Verian said, "Dinner, Renata. It's on the table."

Renata drew a shuddering breath and turned to look at the closed door. "All right, Verian, thanks. We'll be there in a second."

"Eat?" Bart said, incredulous. "Eat, Renata?"

"Of course. As if this conversation had never taken place. It's hard, I know, but I've lived with this a long time. After dinner, we'll make our plans and find some way to get you out of here alive."

Verian waited until Renata and Bart returned to the library and the door was firmly shut, then he went to his own apartment and his private telephone and dialed Russell's number.

"I cooked dinner for them," Verian said, "and they seemed fairly normal, but there's something going on. She's wearing his ring, you know, and when I asked when the wedding was to be he said right away, but she didn't say anything. It could be just a lovers' quarrel, but there's definitely something. They went right back to the library."

Russell said, "I'll tell you what's wrong. Tanner. I saw him yesterday. He's made his contact."

Verian was silent a moment, then he breathed into the mouthpiece. "Then may the good Lord help us all."

"He has," Russell said. "Now, about tonight. Does it look like they're going to stay at home?"

"Yeah, for a while anyway."

"You still refuse to take part in this?"

"Yes."

"Then clear out. Just be sure the door to your apartment is open, and a window, in case she catches the door."

"You don't want to put this off a night or two?"

"No way, not with Tanner in town."

"All right. I'll do what I told you, nothing more."

"Then get on with it. You'd better not plan on sleeping at home tonight."

"Got it," Verian said. "Be seeing you."

13

While Verian finished up in the kitchen, he thought about what he was getting himself into: murder, to put an honest name to it. It made no difference to the law whether or not his was the hand that did the deed. Did he want money that much? Even if the estate his brother had built up came into his possession at the death of his brother's children, he would have Russell. He had to have Russell. He was a wretched businessman. He wouldn't know what to do or how to keep the whole thing from slipping through his fingers, but once everything had been set up. . . . Well, he had no love of Russell Revolo.

The question was the risk. Russell had no respect for law enforcement—for Ed Staple. Russell was a fool.

Verian put the last pot back in its place,

gave the kitchen counter a final wipe, and reached for the light switch.

Yes, the bottom line was the risk. What was the chance of success? Fifty percent? Seventy-five? There were, Verian decided, only two really weak spots. Number one, Russell's over-confidence. Number two, Renata's ability to survive. That last worried him. You couldn't figure Renata, so best not to underestimate her, and Russell tended to do that. It was a gamble, but the odds were in his favor.

Verian stood outside the library door. Inside, Bart was speaking, but he couldn't catch enough to follow the drift. *Cameron,* Verian thought. She was giving the whole thing to Cameron. What were their chances— his and Russell's? Well, say sixty percent for success and ninety against getting caught. Yes, it was worth it, Verian thought, and besides, better death for Renata than Tanner. He turned and went upstairs. He would do his part. *Cameron!* With her gone, who was Cameron?

At twelve o'clock Renata felt totally exhausted. She was sitting in a wing chair that had been her father's favorite and Bart was sprawled in weary dejection on the love seat. She had answered all his questions and listened to his arguments, and they had come full circle back to the starting point: Tanner.

"Now how do we find a way to get you safely out of here?" Renata said.

"When I'm ready I get up and walk out the door, down the front walk, get into my pickup and drive off."

"I don't want you killed right before my eyes."

"You've said several times that he will arrange a clever accident to avoid attention, and I personally believe nothing will happen to me until he's sure he had you."

Renata sighed. "I know. I just don't trust him."

"One thing is settled, you're going to tell all this to Ed Staple. If you don't, I will."

Renata gave an elaborate shrug. "I'll tell him —everything." From the beginning she had intended telling Ed everything, but in the beginning her plans had not included Bart. Bart had been part of the nostalgic memories of an unreclaimable past. "I'll tell him," she repeated, "and he'll put me under twenty-four hour surveillance," which, Renata thought, would make things more difficult for her, and bother Tanner not at all. Aloud she said, "That should amuse Tanner."

"It will keep you safe until we can get a plane out of here for Las Vegas. We can arrange things by telephone and be married within an hour and be on our way to Spain."

"Which will remove us from Ed Staple's jurisdiction and leave us wide open. We wouldn't last a week."

"Renata . . ." Bart began, and then made a hopeless gesture, looked up at the ceiling and sighed.

Renata smiled lovingly. "I know, it's very hard to accept, but there is nothing anyone can do. I'll tell Ed, and he'll tell the sheriff, and it will be just the same as before: my word against Tanner's. You must accept it, darling, it's our only hope."

"Hope of what?"

"That I'll get away and you'll stay alive."

"I can't accept *that*. I won't. There has to be some recourse to law."

"What can the law do? Six years ago I accepted help from an old family friend, Tanner Grimes, who took me to his beautiful mansion in Montecito to train me to be a hostess to valuable clients his company entertained from time to time. Unfortunately, while Tanner was away, I was brutally assaulted by a large man who broke into the premises. I was naturally in a state of shock and terror, so completely demoralized that I attacked Tanner before the medical assistance he called for could arrive, leaving him battered and emasculated. The story makes him look like a saint and me, however understandably and temporarily, mentally unbalanced."

"That story has as many holes as a sieve. They must have believed you, especially after the medical and psychological findings."

"So they believe me. What can they do when my mother drops the suit against Tanner and sends me to a fancy sanitarium for treatment? What can they do when some sadistic nut pours acid in her car? What can *I* do when Tanner threatens me with assorted horrors on a busy street corner? Where is Tanner when these things happen? Who saw him? Who heard him?"

The library was silent. They sat unmoving, looking at each other. A car drove slowly along the street.

"That's him," Renata said.

"We'll get away," Bart said with slow, dogged determination. "We'll find a way to get to him. He's into drugs and prostitution. There has to be a way."

Renata sighed and closed her eyes while she spoke. "My love, I would give my life if it would get you safely out of this. Listen once more, Tanner comes from a fine old California family. His father is dead, but his two sisters married into wealth and political position. Tanner is a dutiful and loyal son to his widowed mother. He keeps her in a lavish Beverly Glen apartment and caters to her every whim. He is a generous contributor to political campaigns and has friends on both sides of the aisle in Sacramento and possibly Washington as well as in county government. To touch him you would be forced to gather irrefutable proof against him. Where is the proof coming from? Are you going to gather it?"

"By damn, yes, if necessary."

Renata opened her eyes and laughed.

The telephone rang.

"Tanner?" Bart asked.

"Probably."

"I'll take it."

"No," Renata was on her feet. "You'll kiss me goodnight and go. I'll take care of everything that I told you I would in the morning. Be careful. Be very, very careful."

The phone rang insistently. She walked into Bart's embrace and lifted her face for his kiss, then walked with him to the front door. The phone continued to ring. When Bart had driven away, Renata walked unhurriedly back to the telephone alcove. She lifted the receiver from the hook and carefully let it drop on the desk top. There was silence, and then the line went dead.

Renata turned and began to climb the stairs. Half way up the first flight she paused, went back down and along the passage to Verian's apartment. She wanted to know: was Verian at home? The connection door was closed. She opened it and went along the enclosed gallery to Verian's apartment door where she knocked. There was no answer. She called, "Uncle Verian!" Receiving no reply, she went in. The living room was almost painfully neat and cold. Verian was not at home.

Renata went to the galley door and looked out into the back garden. The garages were opposite Verian's wing, with the space between mostly given over to a concrete turn around. Beyond was the lawn with its shrubs and borders and the brick paved patio and barbecue area. There was no moonlight. Trees added to the darkness. The old oak at the corner of the kitchen wing turned the shadows beneath it to black velvet. The one dim bulb over the garage hardly penetrated the gloom.

Renata checked the back gallery door, found it unlocked, and turned the bolt, hoping Verian had a key. He shouldn't have left it unlocked. After a while she returned to the entry hall. The receiver was still off the hook. She replaced it. She would be unable to hear it from the third floor. Ed Staple had asked her about the phones.

"There's an extension in Mother's room and in Adolf's," she had told him. "Uncle Verian and the Revolos have their own private lines. There is nothing on the third floor. No one has lived there for the past six years, remember."

"Have one installed immediately," Ed had said.

It had been an order she intended to obey, but there had been no time.

Renata climbed the steep old stairs to the second floor. The door to Adolf's room was open. She stood there a moment looking in, she didn't enter, but went on up to her bedroom and locked the door.

The evening with Bart had left her drained, talked out. If she survived she would one day be glad it was all behind her. She was glad now. She had no energy left for guilt over putting Bart in danger.

Deliberately Renata went to her bedroom window and looked down the street. She made no attempt at concealment, there was no need. If Tanner had the house watched, she saw no one. The street was empty of cars and people.

Renata turned away from the window. She needed sleep. Within five minutes she had slipped between the sheets of her bed, another five and exhaustion had claimed her. She didn't hear the soft sounds as, first the bathroom, and then the door to the cupola stairs were locked, nor did she hear the soft footsteps going down the stairs. In the library the grandfather clock chimed. It was a quarter after one.

The little windup clock with the luminous dial that had been Renata's companion for six years said three minutes after three. Three A.M.? Renata saw the dial through half open eyes. What had disturbed her sleep? She closed her eyes, drifting back. Drifting . . . Her eyelids fluttered. Her nose twitched. That smell. What smell? Smoke.

Smoke!

Renata came awake and upright in bed. She reached for the bedside lamp and switched it on. There it was, curling beneath the door. She threw back the covers and stood beside the bed, her heart racing. Fire, in this old house! She hurried to the closet and fumbled for her old short flannel bathrobe and ran her feet into fuzzy slippers, then she went to the door, turned the key in the lock, and opened the door cautiously. The hall was full of black, acrid smoke.

She slammed the door, leaned against it. What to do? Get out. How? Call for help. The window.

She would open the window and scream. Some neighbor would hear. Renata tugged at the window sash. It didn't budge.

Wedged tight. But how could that be? She had pushed it up with ease only this morning —yesterday morning.

Break it! With what? The straight chair beside the desk. Her hands were on the back when she stopped. If she broke the glass and then opened the door, the open window would pull all the smoke into her room. Oxygen would only feed the fire, wherever it was. A phone! She must get to a phone. What she would give for one in her room now.

She must cover her nose and mouth. Renata hurriedly stripped the slip from her pillow. It would be better if wet. Better yet, get to the bath an soak a towel in water.

Cautiously she opened the bedroom door and clicked on the hall light. The overhead fixture provided little help. Her eyes were instantly burning from smoke. Coughing, choking, she made her blinded way to the bath. Locked!

The door was locked? Impossible! She had used the room only minutes before going to bed. Locked? Stuck?

Renata felt her way to the head of the stairs.

The smoke was so thick she could see nothing. She must reach a phone. She must get out! Where was Verian? He couldn't hear even if she screamed.

The cupola stair. That was the way out. She held her breath and kept the pillow slip over nose and mouth as she fumbled for the cupola door.

She must breathe. She gulped in air and coughed. She found the door, turned the knob and pulled, pulled hard. Nothing happened. Renata dropped the pillowslip to pull with both hands. The door was locked. She was trapped in a burning house.

14

The pillow slip? She had dropped it. Renata
groped about until she found it, and made
her way back to the bedroom. Once inside she
could breathe—and think. But quickly.
Quickly. All that smoke. Where was the fire?
In which room? The stairwell was full of
smoke. The stairs! Impossible. The stairs were
sure death.

Break the window and jump. Better broken
bones than death in a flaming house.
Renata's hand was on the desk chair. She
stopped, turned and looked at her bedroom
door. The window had been nailed shut—
had to be. *Those locked doors*.

All the doors in the house had identical old
fashioned locks. Would one key fit all? That
time long ago when she had lost her room key

they had opened it with a skeleton key from a lock shop. It was worth a try.

With the key from her door, Renata hurried through the roiling smoke to the cupola door. She fumbled the key into the lock. Below there was a small explosion and the sound of shattering glass. *Fire!*

Calm. Be calm.

Renata worked the key gently, pushing forward, pulling back. Almost. There. Carefully she twisted the key. The tumblers in the old lock turned.

It worked!

The door opened. She breathed, coughing at the sudden intake of smoke. Inside the closet-like room, Renata pulled the door shut. Where was the light switch? Found it. A small wall scounce lit her way as she hurried up the winding stairs. With a push, she swung open the trap door and emerged into the cool blackness of the night.

Fresh air. She was safe for now.

But the house! She must get help.

She could take off her slippers and walk down the shingle roof, but there was a drop of a full story between either the kitchen wing and Verian's apartment, or the veranda on the front of the house. The kitchen. It had a full attic and was higher.

Once on the edge she could jump. From the kitchen wing, she could make use of the old oak tree. She had climbed it as a child and knew its branches.

Renata snatched off her slippers and tossed them down, aiming for the puddle of light in front of the garage, where they landed with a small splat of sound.

Now, over the cupola railing. Onto the steep slant of the roof. Easy. Get your bearings. A few steps to be sure.

She could do it!

Using the shape of the oak tree as a guide, Renata let go the railing, and knees bent, moved swiftly down the roof, keeping at an angle. At the edge, she walked along until the ridge of the kitchen wing was beneath her, then sat with her legs hanging over the edge.

How best to do it? Push off? Stand up and jump? For a moment she sat balanced on the edge, then taking a deep breath, she launched herself. Renata landed with one foot on either side of the ridge.

She'd made it, but she teetered. Body bent forward, she reached out to touch the roof and steady herself. A moment later she was running toward the tree.

Don't think. Do it! Jump up!

She had the overhanging branch. Good. Seconds later she had swung herself up and was inching along to the notch where there was a foothold. It was an easy climb to the ground.

Renata retrieved her slippers and stood looking at the house. Except for a light from the upstairs hallway and the faint glow from the cupola hatchway she had forgotten to

close, there was no sign of either fire or
smoke. Well, it was there, probably in the
front of the house.

The fire department.

Call the fire department. From where? The
house was locked up tight. If only she had left
Verian's door open. Her keys. She'd
forgotten her key ring.

A public phone? Not for blocks. She
couldn't drive, her car keys were on her key
ring. A neighbor? Which one? Kettleman.
Over the back fence and rouse George Kettleman.

Renata turned toward the back lawn. A
step or two and she paused. There was movement behind her. She spun to face the
shadows that surrounded the house. A darker
form within the shadows moved, coming
from the side yard.

A moving shape. A man, bent low and
coming swiftly toward her. Too dark! Identification was impossible.

Tanner! The name leaped into her mind.
No. This man was larger.

The man spread his arms as if to grab her.
What was she doing standing here mesmer-
ized? Renata turned and fled toward the back
wall that separated her back yard from
Kettleman's.

Half way across the lawn she tripped on a
sprinkler head, stumbled forward—regained
her balance. Where was he? A quick look
back. Her pursuer kept to the shadows. He

was gaining. She sprinted ahead. Another few seconds—

She had lost a slipper. The patio. A chair against the fence would help. No time.

Renata raced straight ahead toward the gap in the shrubbery where she had handed the cat over the fence to George.

Almost there. Almost. What was that? Oh, no! She heard hard panting breath. He was right behind her.

Renata made a leap and caught the top of the wall, her head and shoulders above the flat concrete cap, her body dangling. She hunched forward, thrusting with her legs. A hand grabbed for her left foot. She screamed and kicked behind her violently. A sharp curse. The second slipper was gone.

Renata squirmed and wiggled her way over the top, screaming with every breath. Her fall into shrubbery on the other side of the fence only increased her frenzy, but in seconds she had rolled free, landing on a strip of lawn, knees bent. She pushed herself upright and ran. The swimming pool was a sheet of dark satin. She skirted it, still screaming, calling for help.

Lights went on upstairs in the house. She didn't see them, but ran on until she was under the roof of the back terrace within reach of the back door. She began pounding on the door while she called George's name. Lights came on downstairs. George was coming. She was safe.

▲ ▲ ▲

On Monday mornings Ed dusted the etagere and the duck decoys displayed on its shelves. The ruddy duck was his favorite and he saved that for last, holding it, turning it, passing his fingers over the wood before putting it back. There was something in the feel of the wood that was elemental—primal—satisfying. As his fingers massaged the ruddy duck, in spite of all his efforts, his thoughts drifted from the pleasant routine task to the Riff case.

Like everything about the case, the fire had that frustrating, things-are-not-what-they-seem quality. There had been a great deal of smoke and not much fire, chiefly because the only open door on the second and third floors was the door to Adolf's room. The electric blanket on Adolf's bed, inadvertently left on, had either shorted out and ignited the blanket and bed linens, or sufficient heat had built up to generate autocombustion. Whatever fire there was, and however short-lived, had been enough to set the mattress smoldering, creating a great deal of toxic smoke. Eventually, oxygen sucked up through the open stairwell had caused the mattress to ignite in a small explosion that had blown out a window. Even with the sudden inflow of outside air, that fire had virtually burned itself out before the firemen arrived.

Ed had talked with the fire station captain, who with a shake of his head, had said these things happen. People forget. They get careless. These people had been careless about checking the smoke detectors. In such an old house the detectors were battery powered, and all of the batteries were dead. They had just been lucky the whole house didn't go. There was absolutely no evidence of arson, although the captain admitted the smoke had seemed unusually dense. And there had been a high acid content in the smoke, not unusual when synthetic fibers were involved such as the blanket and the mattress. Mattresses today were treated with flame retardant materials. Ed was having tests made at the criminology lab.

Ed replaced the ruddy duck on the shelf. That mallard had been his first acquisition. He'd almost forgotten. He moved it a few inches to the right, turning it. No. It was better displayed in the original position. Ed gave the etagere a final wipe and thought of the bookshelves in the Riff library. He couldn't keep his mind off the case.

The phone call had come at a quarter to five Sunday morning. He had phoned Mike before leaving home. When he arrived at the Riff house, the firemen were getting ready to leave. The captain had stayed until Renata had given her account of the fire. Everything seemed to agree except that the firemen hadn't found the third floor bathroom door locked, only a little hard to open. Panic, the captain had said. Not unusual. A person pulled instead of pushed or the reverse. The bottom sash of the bedroom window had worked with ease. There was no explanation for that. Renata had shrugged and said possibly it *had* been locked. The captain had said goodbye and joined his men.

Mike, together with Bart, had arrived at the Riff house then. Renata still in pajamas with the short flannel robe belted around her, had taken them into the library and lighted the fire already laid on the hearth. She had asked George Kettleman to stay while she filled in the missing six years. Ed had asked his questions. She had answered, he thought honestly. Mike had put away his notebook and they were ready to leave.

"I suppose you'll put me under surveillance," Renata had said.

"Yes, ma'am. Twenty-four hours a day until we can get things straightened out. I'd advise you to take my man with you everywhere you go."

"Even to Los Angeles?"

"Yes, ma'am. Even to Los Angeles, and I'd like you to check in with me when you return."

"I'll do that," Bart said. "We appreciate all this, Captain."

Ed folded the dust cloth. Mike Wiley knocked at the open office door, then came in. He was seeing a lot of that taupe vest, Mike thought. The captain was worrying something around. Ed spoke in greeting while he put away the furniture polish and the cloth. They sat across Ed's desk from each other. Ed felt reluctant to begin. It was a devilish, unsatisfying case.

"Well," Ed said at last, "do the alibis stand?"

Mike shrugged. "Lenny swears Verian wasn't out of his sight from the time he left the Riff house until he took Elvira home at twelve. That's not unusual. They entered her apartment house together and Verian didn't leave until six Sunday morning. The neighbors agree. Russell . . . ?" Mike grunted. "Burgess says unless Russell pulled something pretty cute, yes."

"What does Burgess mean by cute?"

"Well, the Revolos have moved into one of the summer beach cottages. They were busy all evening keeping house with all the shades and blinds conveniently open. At 9:36 P.M. they went for a walk on the beach, stopped to chat with a couple believed to live in the neighborhood, and returned to the cottage at 10:08. Lights went out at 10:41."

"Okay, the couple can easily be found to support the alibi. What tipped Burgess?" Ed asked.

"At 11:10 Russell turned on lights on his way to the kitchen for a glass of milk. Burgess could see into the kitchen. Then Russell came out onto the front porch and looked around. Burgess had a comfortable place across the street with the best possible view. At the time he was smoking a cigarette.

He isn't sure he got it out before Russell looked his way."

"Did he move to a new location?"

"Yes, sir. There isn't much cover along there, but he found a recessed doorway. It gave him a pretty good view of the street, there were gaps, but he could still see the beach between Russell's cottage and the one next door so he's sure Russell didn't walk out the back door going in the direction of the yacht club."

Ed said, "To get to town from the other direction he'd have to cross the street. I get the picture."

"Lots of college kids rent those summer places. They had been coming and going all evening. It was Saturday night, remember. At 12:26, a car drove up and four fellows got out. They were feeling good, not rowdy, but not quiet, and after the car drove off, they stood around laughing and talking, crossing the street and coming back before they broke it up, two going to a beach cottage and two to an apartment building across the street.

"Burgess says its possible, if Russell wanted to shake a tail, he could walk along the beach behind a few houses to a path the locals use without Burgess seeing him. It wouldn't be hard to figure there'd be street activity on a Saturday night. All Russell would need to do would be wait for a group and mix in with them to cross the street unnoticed."

Ed turned his head to look out his window. Mike waited.

"There were four fellows?" Ed asked.

"Yes, sir."

"Burgess never saw five?"

"Not at one time, but the guys would split off and then come back. In the dark at half a block away Burgess couldn't swear it was always the same man. They all wore jeans and dark jackets of one kind or another."

Ed grunted. "It's pretty far-fetched at best."

"Cute, Burgess said. *If* he did it."

"It sounds like Russell," Ed admitted, "to pick up on his tail and use it to his advantage."

They were silent in the office.

"So they both have airtight alibis," Ed said. "What about this Tanner Grimes?"

"Quite a story," Mike said. "Quite a story. Do you buy it?"

Ed nodded. "Whole cloth. What did Los Angeles have to say about Tanner?"

"No record, not even a speeding ticket. He's well known in political circles as a heavy contributor, and is high on everybody's most disliked list. L.A. suggests we contact Las Vegas, Tanner spends a lot of time there, but doesn't gamble."

"Where is he now?"

"The same place he was Saturday night, at his mother's Beverly Glenn apartment."

"How about known associates?"

"How about the current list of Who's Who in Southern California? No close personal friends."

"Employees?"

"A housekeeper/cook at his Newport Beach condo and a valet, houseman, chauffeur. The cook is permanent, the housemen average about a year each. He has a secretary in his downtown L.A. office who runs the place. The businesses all seem to be legit. He's worth a bundle and it looks like he's squeaky clean, just unpopular."

Ed looked at his window without seeing the view. Tanner had no connection with the fire. Renata dead wasn't what he wanted if you believed the story as told, and Ed did. Tanner only added urgency to Verian's and Russell's need. They had to be kept as separate entities from Tanner.

A picture was forming, Ed thought. Verian and Russell he saw clearly, Tanner he could understand. It was Renata who remained out of focus. He was beginning to see, but belief in the shape of the fuzzy images was slow to develop. What did Mike think, Ed wondered. Was he ready to translate his own suspicions into words? He decided not yet, but turned from the window to face Mike.

"What did the sheriff say, Captain?" Mike asked.

Ed grinned and shrugged. "About what you'd expect. What can he say?"

"He remembered the case, didn't he?"

"Yeah. He knew both families. Old Man Grimes had been active in the sheriff's first campaign and since then Tanner has made generous contributions. The Riveras' political affiliations run more to the state level so the personal ties with the Grimes' are stronger. The sheriff was glad when the case was dropped."

Mike laughed. "Must have been like a gift from heaven. Where does he stand now?"

"He's sure he can rely on my discretion in finding the truth," Ed said.

Mike shook his head and turned his eyes toward the ceiling. "Not exactly carte blanche. So what's the next move?"

"That's just it," Ed said. "Right now I'm not sure who's carrying the ball. All we can hope is that we can read the signals right. Do you have any inspired guesses?"

Mike shook his head. "I'd say the player to watch is Renata."

Ed nodded, thinking that they were on the same track. "Let's hope we can keep her under surveillance."

Verian took his favorite glass from among the odds and ends that had accumulated on the kitchen shelves. It was a footed Libby's water tumbler in a clear, thin glass. He filled it with ice, put in a slice of lemon, took a bottle of mineral water from the refrigerator and went to his own living room, where he settled himself comfortably with the telephone in easy reach. Verian poured the mineral water and waited for the glass to bead before he dialed Russell's office number. As prearranged, it was five minutes to twelve noon.

When Russell answered, Verian said, "They've gone into Los Angeles about their passports so we can talk. The house is a mess for nothing. Renata managed to save the front door by breaking a window but the whole place is a shambles—smoke—water— they drug the mattress out. It's awful."

Russell sighed. "I know and I'm sorry. The smoke was terrible. I couldn't have made it to unlock the bathroom door or pull the nail out of her bedroom window without a gas mask. Why didn't you tell me about the keys? I could have fixed the cupola door and we would have had her if I'd known one worked on all doors."

"How could I tell you," Verian said. "I didn't know myself."

"That damn woman has more lives than any ten cats."

"And as far as I'm concerned, she'll go on living. I'm telling you, Russell . . ."

"Hold on a minute," Russell said and Verian waited until the voices from Russell's office died away.

"Listen, Verian, there's a developer I do the bookkeeping for who will give us a million for that beach front property if we can deliver title in the next six months. Plus, there's a couple of fellows interested in that lemon orchard as a subdivision. That could bring in almost half a million, leaving all the rest of the estate intact for later. Now, when can we get together? I've got an idea."

"What?" Verian demanded. "Burn the

whole house down?"

"No. We'll set up Tanner and let him take the fall."

"We'll what?"

"Set up Tanner. . . ."

"Russell, I told you before, that's a crazy scheme. Set up Tanner? Tanner! Great Jehosephat! No thanks. I'm too young to die."

Verian carefully replaced the receiver on the hook. He sipped his mineral water. A million and a half, Verian thought. Tanner will get her this time, not even Ed Staple could help her.

A million and a half. And after Tanner got her, it would all just sit there for another seven years because nobody would be able to find her where Tanner would take her—or her body if he killed her. Even then, it would go to Cameron.

By the great Jehosephat, no! Not if he had to do it himself.

Verian stretched out in his chair, legs extended, head resting on the high back, and closed his eyes. How? How, so he wouldn't get caught. He couldn't just shoot her. Or could he? There was Augustin's old gun. A thirty-eight revolver, he thought. Where was it now? Probably still in the drawer of the night stand on what had been Augustin's side of the bed. Yeah. That's where it was. What about shells? Along with the gun, most likely.

The phone rang. Russell said, "I've taken the afternoon off. I'm coming over."

15

Bart parked the Mercedes at the curb in front of the Riff house behind a blue Chrysler sedan. The front door of the house was open and Verian was talking to a man in a dark blue suit. Bart got out and walked around to open the car door for Renata. They stood on the curb watching the men talking with gestures that suggested an argument. The man in the suit shrugged and turned to walk away, leaving Verian, dressed in black and white checked trousers, his white chef's jacket and hat, staring after him.

"I wonder what has Uncle Verian so riled up," Renata said. "He looks about ready to explode." As the man walked toward them, Renata said, "I should know who that is."

"Insurance," Bart said. "DeMeer Insurance Agency."

"Of course, I remember. I told Uncle Verian to call and have them out to appraise the fire damage."

With a curt nod in their direction, DeMeer strode around to the driver's side of his car, got in, and drove away. Renata started up the walk toward the waiting Verian.

"What did DeMeer say?" Renata asked.

Verian shook a defiant fist at the disappearing sedan. "Wait. That's what he said, wait for the appraisal. He told me to leave everything just as it is. Don't touch a thing." Verian threw up his hands in a gesture of outraged defeat, stalked down the entry and into the living room. "Stinks," he said, throwing himself into his favorite chair, "the whole house stinks. How does he expect anyone to live with such a stench for a week? He said ten days, but I raised such hell he agreed to a week." Verian sat back, eyes snapping in anger. "Mix me a drink, Bart."

"Sure." Bart grinned. "What do you want?"

"I don't know, I don't drink. Just fix me something."

"How about a bourbon and water?"

"Okay, just make it strong." Verian folded his arms across his chest and glared at Renata. "Who does he think he is, that DeMeer. I had Canaan and Pete coming in tomorrow to help me get started on this mess. I'll tell you, Renata, there's nothing in this house that doesn't smell of smoke, even the rooms that were closed off. It's into everything."

Verian turned his head away, and Renata thought from the heave of his shoulders, that he was going to cry.

"Well, a week isn't so long, Uncle Verian, and it could have been a lot worse. All that's really lost is Adolf's bed and the carpet. That's too bad, because it was one of the best Orientals, but even that may be salvageable if you turn it around. It's mostly scorch."

Verian unfolded his arms to accept his drink. "I know," he said, "it's just that . . ." He took a sip of his drink and blew out a sigh. "It's just that . . . well, who would think with all the doors closed such a little fire could do so much damage?"

Renata smiled and thought, *And all for nothing. I didn't die trying to escape.* Aloud she said, "It will clean up, Uncle Verian, and I'm sure it's better to wait for the appraiser," and then to change the subject, she asked if he had prepared dinner.

"No. I've got the makings for a quick meal, some chops, and I made a charlotte russe for dessert. I wasn't sure when you'd be home, or if you'd want to eat here."

Bart handed Renata her usual glass of white wine and sat beside her on the sofa, a tall drink in his hand.

"Sounds great, Verian," Bart said. "We've had a pretty tiring day."

Renata let the conversation drift over the events of the day before she said, "You'd better check in with Ed Staple, Bart. He knows we're home, but you said you'd call in."

Bart had left the room, Verian finished his drink and was about to follow, when Renata stopped him.

"Uncle Verian, did I get any phone calls today?"

Verian gave her a questioning look and a smile. "Yeah, I almost forgot. Some old fellow called and said tell you everything you wanted was ready, to let him know when. And another guy called, said he'd have to talk to you and he'd be back between eleven and midnight. Seems like I should know the old fellow."

"Mr. Tobias," Renata said. "You might remember him."

"Toby? Sure. Haven't seen him since your dad died, but sure, I remember Toby."

"Well, I asked him to run some errands for me today while I was in the city."

Renata smiled and sipped her wine, and presently Verian said, "Dinner in about forty minutes," and left the living room.

Bart stood in the doorway. "Captain Staple wants to talk to you Renata."

She nodded and put down the wine glass. As she passed Bart, she paused a moment to kiss him. "I'll just be a minute," she said.

Ed said, "Welcome home, Miss Riff. I understand you had a pleasant day."

"Thank you, we did."

"I wanted to let you know your Uncle

Verian and Russell Revolo have established alibis for themselves for Saturday night. Verian's seems straight. Russell's is open to question but there is nothing definite. My men found small nail holes in your bedroom window and indications that the nails were removed with some kind of pliers. We are checking into that. The captain at the fire station states positively no one could have entered the house and gone through the smoke without a gas mask. Also any clothing worn at that time would be impregnated with smoke fumes.

"As to the man in the yard, my personal opinion is that he was in no way connected with Tanner Grimes. Mr. Grimes has been staying with his mother in her apartment for the past several nights and was with her on Saturday night.

"Until we can establish a provable connection between the window being nailed shut, the locked doors, and the man in the back yard, I would strongly advise you, Miss Riff, not to be too trusting of anyone close to you. Further, should you wish to leave the house alone, tell the detective on duty outside your home your intended destination, please."

Renata said, "Thank you, Captain Staple," and let a little time pass before she said, "I agree that Tanner had nothing to do with the fire. It isn't his style, nor would it accomplish his purpose." After another pause, she added, "It may amuse you and Detective Wiley to know that my uncle is very upset over the condition of the house and finds it difficult to believe that such a little fire caused so much damage. He is a meticulous housekeeper."

Ed chuckled. "Tell your uncle should he need someone to clean and refurbish any antiques, I know just the man. I'll tell Detective Wiley. I am pleased to know you are cognizant of the situation. I will keep you informed, Miss Riff."

Renata remained at the telephone alcove for a long moment before returning to the living room and Bart. She had been right about Ed Staple. He was very good at puzzle solving and given the pieces he would not rest until he had fit them together to make a picture. So much for you, Tanner, she thought, and so much for you Russell. Uncle Verian . . . About Verian she felt sorry.

Renata stood at the front window and watched until Bart exchanged places between the Mercedes and his pickup and drove from the garage back onto the street. He waved as he passed. An old brown-over-tan Buick slid out from the opposite curb and fell into place behind the pickup. Renata smiled. Bart would be as safe as Ed Staple could make him. Now it was time to look out for herself.

Renata went to the small living room bar and looked through the bottles. Bailey's Original Irish Cream had been Audrey Revolo's after dinner drink. She selected an old fashioned glass of cut crystal, dropped an ice cube and poured in enough liqueur to cover them, then put the glass on the black lacquer cabinet beside Verian's usual chair. She didn't sit down, but went back to stand at the window. Her plan of escape was simple. It would get her out of Port Haven and safely to the Santa Barbara airport at Goleta, but it would leave a trail. She had no illusions about that. She would be lucky if Tanner didn't have someone in San Francisco to intercept her before she could get another flight out. She had made the plans with Bart in mind. The important thing was to remove him from jeopardy, but since the fire she had had second thoughts.

If she could save Bart, and at the same time set herself free—she would lose Bart, but if she were believed dead . . . She would be dead if Tanner caught her, she had seen to that, she would not be his slave. She had to think. Renata returned to the club chair and sat down. She swirled the liqueur in the glass, looking at it, but not drinking.

Ten minutes passed. Fifteen. The grandfather clock chimed the half hour. She would need Mr. Tobias again, and it would help if she knew something of Verian's plans. Maybe she could guess, but . . .

Did it matter? Wouldn't it be better if the plans were hers? She would need to be in control. A talk with Verian, perhaps? What time was it? She looked at her watch. Twenty-five until eleven. Verian watched television. She would go and see.

Outside Verian's door she paused to listen. The television was on. She knocked and called, "Uncle Verian, can we talk?"

"Door's not locked," Verian said.

Renata went in and sat down, glad she had kept her suit jacket on, the room was unnecessarily chilly. Verian pressed the remote control button and the TV screen went to black.

Verian said, "I appreciate your attitude about me leaving that blanket on."

Renata waved a dismissing hand. "I know how you feel about the house. Forget it. Take the best offer the insurance appraiser makes and do what needs to be done that the insurance doesn't cover. Ed Staple said tell you he knows a man who can clean any of the antiques."

"Well, it was still a damn fool thing to do," Verian said, "but I'll see that everything is cleaned and repainted."

"I'm not worried about that. I wanted to talk about other things."

"Okay. Have at it."

"Tanner's back. I didn't know if you knew."

"Yeah, I heard about that. Russell saw him in Santa Barbara. I'm sorry, Renata. What are you going to do? Both Alva and Adolf are dead now."

"There's Bart. Tanner has told me not to marry if I want Bart to live."

Verian's eyebrows lifted. "He's talked with you then."

"Oh, yes. I expect he'll make his move very

soon. I'll have to run, of course, so there are some things I think you'd better know."

"Any way I can help?"

"Thanks, Uncle Verian, I appreciate that, and I'll let you know. Maybe you can. I'm going to ask one of the fishing boat captains to smuggle me out at night. I'll have to set it up, and I may need someone to cover me."

"I'll do what I can."

"Dad had an old gun, didn't he?"

Verian's head jerked and his eyes flicked over her. So he'd thought about that. It was the natural next move. To be safe, she'd better have Mr. Tobias get her some blanks, thirty-eights, if she remembered right.

"I wouldn't want you to hurt anybody, but I'd feel better if I had some protection. Nothing's settled yet, I'll have to get back to you."

"What about Staple? Did you tell him about Tanner?"

"Yes, everything. I'll have to slip out. Tanner would spot a tail."

Verian nodded. "Well, let me know."

Renata sat silent, looking at him, smiling at him, remembering other times. She gave herself a shake. Yesterday was irretrievable. Today her Uncle Verian was her enemy. She wondered, did he know about the new will? Most probably. Russell, she thought. Russell, that insidious devil.

"I will need to move fast, Uncle Verian," she said. "I'll give you the details very soon."

She stood and went to him, looking down at

his relaxed figure. Then, on impulse, she bent down and kissed him on the forehead. That, she told herself, was for the good times. She said, "I always loved you, Uncle Verian. I'll miss you."

His look of surprise was almost comical. Renata stood smiling down at him for a moment, said good night, and left the room.

It was too late to phone Mr. Tobias. That must wait until morning, besides she wasn't sure of everything yet, but from her conversation with Verian she felt positive she must act soon. Verian knew about Tanner, and probably about the will, and mention of her father's old revolver had brought a guilty response. How did they plan to do it? The vital thing for both Verian and Russell was, don't get caught. How could they work it? How . . . ?

Oh no! They wouldn't. They wouldn't dare! But of course Russell would. He had no understanding of Tanner. Russell would think *he* could set up *Tanner*.

But Verian? Verian understood. Could Russell persuade him? What bait would Russell use? Money? The estate? Russell would make the stakes high and take the risks and Verian would be unable to resist the gamble.

That was it. They planned to set Tanner up for the fall. Renata stopped at the bottom of the stair and looked back toward Verian's apartment. She laughed. *They planned to make Tanner their fall guy.* Of course they did, and she was going to help them.

Renata ran lightly up the stair. It was time to get out of her city clothes and into jeans and sweatshirt. Time to meet Henry Costus and arrange about the fishing boat.

Halfway up the second flight she stopped suddenly. She had it! All those days and nights of thinking—thinking, planning, discarding plan after plan—had come together in one blindingly bright moment of insight. It would be risky, very risky, and a great deal would depend on her judgement of Ed Staple, but the risks didn't matter—not at all.

Renata went slowly up the remaining steps, her mind busy with details. If it worked she would be free—free now and forever. *And*—she would have Bart.

16

Only Verian's eyes moved as he watched Renata leave his apartment. For a while he didn't think. To think would be to remember. For a time he managed to see nothing but the door she had closed behind her, a little girl of a woman, petite and pretty. His glance moved to the closed Venetian blind covering the gallery window, but the memories came. There was no way he could shut them out.

Alva hadn't been pleased to add her brother-in-law to her household. At the end of his first month in this house there had been some words, and after they were over, when he had gone to his room, there had been a knock at the door, just like tonight. The door had opened and Renata had come in wearing her nightgown and a warm fuzzy robe. She had put her arms around him and kissed his cheek and said she loved him and not to go away.

Verian's hand went up, his fingers touching the spot Renata had kissed tonight. The incident came back to him in all its detail, along with some other things Renata had done. The memories didn't make him happy. They didn't change anything, still he put off telephoning Russell as he must. This was a break they hadn't counted on. It was going to make things a lot easier—and a lot harder.

The glow from the outside light over the kitchen door penetrated the closed blinds of the gallery window. What now, Verian wondered? He got up and pulled open a slit to look out. Renata came out into the back yard dressed in her old Levi's and that battered nylon jacket she had arrived home in. She went directly to the section of the garage where the Mercedes was housed, and within a couple of minutes she was backing out.

Verian left his post at the window and hurried into the living room where he could see which direction she took. She paused beside a blue Chrysler Cordoba and talked with the man sitting inside, then she drove off with the blue Cordoba following. She was going to the wharf to make arrangements for the getaway boat. It was time to call Russell. Verian smiled and chuckled, he hoped Russell would be asleep. Russell hated to have his sleep disturbed.

* * *

Renata paused before going upstairs. The interview with Henry Costus about a getaway boat had been about as she expected. It had been necessary to tell Henry more than she really wanted to, but the arrangements had been made. Henry had taken her aboard the *Spring Tide* and checked her out at the controls. Everything had gone smoothly, but only because the detective in the blue Cordoba had been an ever present shadow. There had been other shadows.

How had Tanner known? Renata turned to look at the telephone alcove. Bugged? More likely the line had been tapped. She should have thought of that. What else had she missed? The police radio frequency? Beyond a doubt. There had been no attempt at secrecy about the surveillance, it was just there. Very convenient from Tanner's point of view, it saved him manpower and provided better information.

All right, what had she said over the phone that was useful? Neither the original contact with Henry nor Mr. Tobias had been made here, although both men had called in. If Verian hadn't recognized Mr. Tobias, then neither would Tanner, so Mr. Tobias was safe. Henry wouldn't be on the wharf tomorrow night, so she need not worry about him. That was all right, then.

Renata began to mount the stairs. How much should she tell Ed? What did she want Tanner to know? Verian would have contacted Russell, was it possible Tanner had tapped Verian's line? Probable, since the fire had doubtless shown Tanner that Verian and Russell had reason to want her dead. She wouldn't worry about that so long as Verian had no reason to suspect.

There were still things to do, but first a few hours sleep. Her mind was tired. Her body was tired. Time. The timing. She had to fit it all together, otherwise it wouldn't work.

At seven o'clock the next morning, Renata sat at the kitchen table with her toast and coffee while Verian poached eggs and made toast for himself.

Renata said, "I want you to understand, Uncle Verian, this is going to be dangerous. I don't want you to expose yourself at all, but I've worked that out. If you're willing to take the chance, I'll spell it out for you."

Verian transferred his eggs to a Haviland sauce dish and put his toast on a matching breakfast plate. "Let's go into the breakfast room. I don't like eating in the kitchen."

Verian put everything on a tray and carried it into the adjoining room.

"Now," he said, when they were settled, "tell me how you plan to pull this off, then I'll make a decision."

As briefly as possible, Renata outlined her scheme. She would take the *Spring Tide* to the Goleta Beach pier where Henry would meet her with a borrowed car. Henry would row himself back to the *Spring Tide* in the dingy Renata had used to get ashore, and she would take the car to the airport at Goleta.

"Henry will have a disguise and an airline ticket in the car. It's chancy. Tanner will be watching the airport, but I'll wear a wig and makeup, and I'll be driving in from the north in a car with a San Luis Obispo dealer's license guard. I'll make it."

"How are you going to get on board the *Spring Tide*?" Verian asked.

"Well, it's complicated," Renata said. "First we'll have to shake Ed's surveillance, then once we get to the wharf area I'll need you to cover for me while I run for it."

In detail, Renata explained her plan for getting on board the *Spring Tide*.

"It's crazy," Verian said. "You'll never make it. Why don't I just drive you up to the *Spring Tide*'s mooring and you get on board and go?"

"Because Tanner knows about Henry and the boat. I'm sure he had men on the wharf last night. He would spot a car the moment it hit Harbor Boulevard. You wouldn't get half a block before he'd have you blocked off and I'd be gone. He would love it. I'll have to make a run for it as I outlined. That will take about a minute. It will take another two minutes to slip the dock lines and get on board, then another couple to pull far enough away so a good broad jump wouldn't put him on the deck. I have to prevent that happening. That's why I want you on the wharf with Dad's old thirty-eight and a good safe cover.

You won't need to do anything but fire at random to keep them at the distance long enough for me to get away from the pier."

"What about Staple's men?"

"Tanner will have them spotted and take care of them, you can count on that."

"You mean kill them?"

"Of course not. A sap, or a chloroform cloth, a micky in a drink, some diversion—lots of possibilities."

"Won't Staple take that into consideration?"

"Certainly. There'll be backup units, but he can do only so much, and he has to be law abiding. Anyway, it's all a matter of timing. I need five minutes at most, and with luck, four."

Verian poured fresh coffee for himself and Renata.

She said, "The time I'll be most vulnerable is making the run and slipping the dock lines. I'll have to run along the edge of the wharf to make the best time and I'll be in the open. Surprise will give me a few seconds lead and with you pinging away, I should make it. Anyway, it's my best shot. Ed can't keep up this surveillance forever, and the minute that's gone, so am I."

Verian sipped his coffee. The setup was too perfect. He couldn't have planned it better himself. What was she up to? But then, when you thought it through it was about as good a scheme as possible. It was amazing how she had covered all the angles. And she sure knew Tanner.

Verian let his thoughts drift back to the days before Augustin had bailed him out. He knew Tanner's kind. Relentless, that's what they were. They never gave up. You never got off, it made a bad example.

She was right about Staple. A couple more days, that was all he could give her. Time to marry Bart and get away. But she couldn't marry Bart. She had to run.

If he could figure this, Verian thought, so could Tanner. So what were the chances the scenario would play the way she laid it out? Was she setting him up? If she was he didn't see it. It was a gamble. Were the stakes high enough? A million right off and money—a steady supply of money, once the estate was set up. And Russell out front to take the heavy chances, against—against what? A nice quiet, comfortable—respectable—life here in Port Haven. So all right, he'd do it. The ultimate gamble. Go for broke.

Verian looked at Renata sitting, sipping coffee, patiently waiting. Too bad. Things could have been very different for her except for those few wild weeks of rebellion.

"Okay, honey. I'll cover for you."

"Great. Thanks, Uncle Verian. I'll make this up to you. I won't forget."

She got up and gave him a smile. "I've got some things to do. Will you fix dinner for Bart and me tonight?"

"Sure. You go ahead. I'll see that things are set for tonight."

Renata waited until she had reached the safety of her room before she let out the big sigh and allowed herself to relax. *He had bought it.* It was set up. She knew what Verian would do. While he shopped for food he would call Russell. They wouldn't need to meet until after she had helped Verian slip by Ed's surveillance. It was a perfect setup for them. Too perfect, really, but the chance had paid off.

Now she would have to contact Mr. Tobias about the blanks. Verian would give the gun to Russell and Russell probably had never held a revolver in his hand. Anything could happen with live ammunition. He could kill somebody. Renata laughed. Gruesome, but funny in a way.

There were other things to do, most of which could be done by phone. She would make a call or two from home to keep Tanner from worrying. The rest she would make from Kettleman's. She would be forced to break in, but George always left a window open a few inches for Sir Thomas. A nice cat, Sir Thomas. He had been a true friend and a real help.

She had time to kill. That word kept cropping up. Had she miscalculated somewhere? Maybe she'd go down to Alva's bathroom and have a long, soothing tub bath instead of a shower. She should review things, and maybe later she should check in with Ed Staple.

Mike Wiley sat in the chair across the desk from Ed. The office was quiet after a series of detectives had made their reports.

"Looks like she intends to make a run for it aboard Henry Costus' fishing boat," Mike said.

"Run to where?" Ed said. "Nobody's seen Henry this morning. His wife says she doesn't know where he is, only that he will be back sometime before tomorrow morning."

"Well, he made no secret about it. He said Renata was in a spot of trouble and he had agreed to loan her his boat whenever she needed it. He said he couldn't do less for an old friend."

"I know. That's probably all we'll get out of him. It's his business. We'll probably get the same answer from Renata."

"You want me to get her on the phone?"

"No, I think the boys are right, the phone's been tapped and our radio frequency is being picked up. What happened to the wedding? Where is Bart? Why isn't he taking her off on a honeymoon?"

"The passports," Mike said.

"I know. We're all waiting for the passports." Ed turned to look at his collection of duck decoys. They brought him no joy today. "Damn we can't keep this up forever. We've got half the force on the Riff case now."

"Maybe we won't have to," Mike said. "There's too much stirring. Something's bound to happen soon."

"Yeah," Ed agreed, "things are working and from the feel of it, Renata is pulling the strings."

Ed swiveled his chair so that he looked out the west window. Mike waited, and presently, Ed said, "Call John Silas and find out if the new will has been signed."

Ed continued to stare out the window while Mike made the call.

"It's a long complicated will," Mike reported, "and it won't be ready for her signature until tomorrow."

"Has he heard from her?" Ed asked.

"Not in the last few days."

"Has she given John any instructions regarding the will should she be prevented from signing it?"

"No. All her instructions should something happen to her are in a sealed envelope in a safety deposit box to be delivered to John in the event of her death or disappearance."

Ed let out a groaning sigh. "She's thought of it all, hasn't she? Tell John thanks. There's probably a holographic will instructing Bart to carry out her wishes as stated in the unsigned will. Maybe someone should tell Verian."

"Do you think they will try something tonight?"

"I think Renata will."

"You think she'll make a run for it aboard the *Spring Tide*, Captain?"

Ed swiveled away from the window and

met Mike's inquiring gaze, "I wish I thought that was all she had in mind. She's in love. This time escape won't be enough. This time she wants her freedom."

17

They were as far apart as the Riff living room permitted. Renata was curled up on one end of the sofa, while Bart stood at the front bay window.

"Bart, I wish you wouldn't stand at the window," Renata said. "There's no need making a target of yourself."

"A shot from the street would be out and out murder, Renata. If you have done anything, you have convinced me that quick death isn't Tanner's intent."

Bart left the window and crossed the room to stand in front of Renata. "The only solution to this is for us to get married and get out of here. We can establish ourselves somewhere under a different name if necessary."

Renata sighed. "Okay, my darling, let's get married. We have the license, don't we?"

"Yes."

"Then we do it, but we stay. At least here someone will investigate our deaths. Here, there's a chance Tanner wouldn't get away with it. Once we leave this police jurisdiction, we're sitting ducks. There is nothing any law enforcement body can do before the fact, Bart. Believe me, Tanner will find us, then who is going to bring charges when I disappear? I'm just a stranger who vanishes without a trace. And who is going to question the accident that takes your life? Even your parents can't know your new identity, it would put them in jeopardy."

"What you're saying is this marriage would be a death pact."

"Just about."

"I can't accept that."

"You must. We've run out of time."

So, Renata thought, we've come full circle again . . . They had had some moments. In a way, more than most. There had been no room for sham or pretense or the games people play. She had to give this thing that had happened between them substance. She had to win. The scheme had to work.

"I must make a run for it, Bart," Renata said. "You were a dream. A normal life was a lovely dream I should never have allowed myself to indulge in. I can get away—alone. That's my only hope, and yours. It's the best I can do for now. Given a little time, things may change. That's what I'm counting on. What I'm asking is, will you wait? Will you give me the necessary time?"

Bart flopped into Verian's favorite chair. He looked at Renata through half closed eyes, dejection in every line of his body. What had she done to him? Look at him. Miserable, unhappy, defeated. She couldn't even go to him, no matter how she longed to hold him close to reassure and comfort him. She dare not touch him. The need was too strong, once given in to, desire would have its way.

"How much time, Renata?" Bart asked. "We've lost six years already."

Renata's smile was a little crooked and the look that came into her eyes was strange to Bart. For a moment she seemed savage. The expression vanished so swiftly Bart wasn't sure he had seen it.

"True," she said, "we have a lot of catching up to do."

She wasn't meeting his glance, but was looking off through the window. I've lost her, Bart thought. Even if I got her, I wouldn't have her. If I force the marriage . . . ? Could I protect her? No. I would only sacrifice myself. If we run together . . . How much time could we buy? How much happiness? How much security?

It was a no win situation, unless . . . ! Unless something happened to Tanner. Okay, say she made good her escape, where would that leave Tanner? Here, or in Los Angeles. Accidents did happen.

He was kidding himself. He wouldn't know how to go about faking an accident. And he couldn't deliberately kill anybody. Not and live with himself. Even if he managed it and she came back, Tanner would still be between them.

It was a dead end street. He had to let her go. He had no choice. She would get away with her life, and that was something.

"When?" Bart asked.

"It will have to be soon. Ed can't keep us under surveillance much longer. He's waiting for the passports. Hang onto them when you get them. I'll find a way to get in touch. We'll have our honeymoon. Who knows, Tanner's kind can't last forever. Anyway, we have tonight."

Renata patted the place beside her on the sofa, and after a moment, Bart came to occupy it.

Renata looked at her watch: one-fifteen. Perfect. Everything was done. Mr. Tobias had come through with all she had asked of him. Verian—? She wasn't too sure of Verian. He seemed at first to have accepted her scheme, but as the day progressed she had seen him pause in what he was doing to watch her. Well, he was a gambler. He must have weighed his chances of success against the cost of failure just as she had. The question was, how was he hedging his bets?

It was time. She left the lights on in her room to be visible from the street, and hurried down the stairs and along to Verian's room where she knocked lightly on the door.

Then she slipped out into the back yard and called softly to the detective on duty there. There was an immediate response.

"Miss Riff, is that you?"

"Yes. I know it's an impossible hour, and Bart only left here a short time ago, but I need to call him, and I don't want to attract attention. It's kind of important, and if I don't do it now, I'll have to wait until he comes home from work tomorrow and that will make a whole day's delay. I don't want to make the call from the house. Could you drive me down to the pay phone at the gas station?"

"I'll have to check in," the detective said.

"I'll wait."

Would Ed buy it? Would he think that if he didn't agree she would make the call from the house anyway? The detective returned in a moment and said it was okay, for her to get into his car. They were gone fifteen minutes, time enough for Verian to get safely over the back wall and out through George Kettleman's front garden gate. Renata said her thanks to the detective and went upstairs. She turned on the lights in her bathroom for long enough to change into jeans and shirt and put on the old nylon jacket. A quick check of the pockets to be sure she had forgotten nothing, and everything was waterproof. She was ready.

The lights went out and Renata made her way through the darkened house to Verian's apartment. His bedroom window was always open. Swinging out the old wooden frame screen made only the slightest sound, she slipped through, dropping to the ground on the side lawn. The neighbor's fence was twelve feet away. She had loosened three pickets while Verian shopped, now she moved them aside and edged her way through. In half a minute she was over the back fence, and three minutes later she had skirted around the house next door to Kettleman's, crossed the street, and was slipping into the seat of the compact car Mr. Tobias had rented, where Verian waited.

At Renata's direction, Verian drove through old back streets until they came out on Reyes Street far down near its end and drove back until they had crossed the railroad spur, where Renata directed him to park.

"You understand the layout, don't you, Uncle Verian?" Renata asked.

"Well," Verian said, "basically."

"Okay, once again. Reyes runs behind Harbor Boulevard. It's one of a couple of short streets between Harbor and the railroad and the freeway. When you leave, go straight down to Padre Boulevard and back to town. Don't try to go back the way I brought you."

"I understand that."

"The alley I'm going to use is about a half block further on. You go back across the railroad spur and down to Billings Lane. That will bring you out in front of the Marsden

Cannery buildings. Cross over, walk around the cannery to the wharf and along the wharf until you are as near the *Spring Tide* as you can get and find good cover. Stay there. I'll give you time, then I'll make my run. Everything clear?"

"Yeah. I got it."

"Thanks, Uncle Verian. You're probably saving my life."

Verian's face was a pale oblong, but she could see that he was smiling. "If I've helped, I'm very glad. Good-bye, Renata, and I wish you the best of luck."

Renata slipped out of the car and in seconds had blended into the gloom of the poorly lighted streets. A minute passed before a man's figure moved from the opening into the railroad spur and came swiftly toward the car where Verian waited. The car door opened and Russell slid into the seat Renata had occupied. Verian repeated the instructions Renata had given him.

"You're sure you can handle this?" Verian said.

"I borrowed a hand gun and practiced with it a little. I can aim and fire. I'll have to be lucky. How many shells?"

"I asked one of the boys about the gun. You're lucky there. It's a revolver, not an automatic. There are six shells in the chamber, but it has a pretty long range for a hand gun, which means you won't have to get too close. Now we'd better go, she has this thing timed to the last second. Just be sure

Tanner's men are visible before you fire."

The gate that closed off the crooked service alley that looked as if it ended at the back door of Sandy's Bar was a triangle made of cast iron pipe. All she had to do was duck under. The alley turned and went all the way through, dead ending at the Chandlery building. Beyond the Chandlery was the paved railroad spur that angled through to the dock. Between the Chandlery and the smaller building next door was a drainage gutter. It was only a few feet wide, but it gave access to Harbor Boulevard. She would come out a few doors east of Gil's Bar.

Renata ducked under the gate and took a few quick strides, keeping close to the wall. The back door of Sandy's Bar opened, spilling light into the alley. Renata turned her back, leaned against the wall and made wretching sounds. Bottles rattled, the door clicked shut, the only light was a dim bulb over Sandy's door.

She turned the corner into the full length of the alley. Further along, beneath another dim light bulb, a dog pulled at papers, searching for food. She approached slowly, spoke calmly and walked by, keeping close against the opposite wall.

There was better light over the Chandlery's back service entrance. Renata moved quickly, and disappeared into the narrow slit of the drainage gutter. At the edge of the sidewalk along Harbor, she paused, flattened herself against the west wall and looked out toward the Marsden Cannery, then turned her head to look the other way.

The bars were closing, the stragglers coming out one by one. If there was surveillance on the street, it was invisible.

The door of Gil's Bar opened. A voice said, "You sure you can make it, Mel? I can get you a taxi."

Mel said, "I can make it. Don't you worry about ole Mel. Ole Mel will make it."

Ole Mel made his unsteady way across the street toward a parked pickup truck. The door of Gil's Bar closed. Mel's pickup moved away from the curb, heading toward Padre Avenue. Down toward the Marsden Cannery, two figures crossed the street, one a few seconds behind the other. As soon as the two figures disappeared, Renata left the protection of the drainage gutter and slouched unevenly, but quickly across the street, along in front of the two buildings opposite, and around them to the open wharf. She paused in the shadow of the buildings, moved along their walls to a stack of fish boxes, and looked over the scene before her.

There was sufficient light fog to soften the lights, but it wasn't heavy enough to hide anyone moving. The Marsden lights at the far end of the wharf were brightest, but far enough away to be no worry. The first finger of pier where the fishing boats were tied up was fifty yards away, the railroad spur another fifty. There were outside lights over the two fish sheds, but nothing over a string of vacant buildings.

Where were they, Renata wondered, Ed's men and Tanner's? She could guess about Tanner's. They would be on board the *Spring Tide*, waiting. She would need to draw them off. Would Ed's men have spotted them? Sure. They were somewhere along the buildings, in the shadows of the railroad spur, on board a neighboring fishing boat, a police launch standing handily off shore. She shouldn't keep them waiting any longer. Russell and Verian would be in place, it was time to make the run.

Renata left the shelter of the fish boxes and ran lightly to the open edge of the wharf, where she turned to run toward the pier and the *Spring Tide*. She ran easily, not sprinting, but moving with a smooth, even stride.

Nothing moved. The only sound was the slap of the waves against the pilings. Then she heard it, the sound she had been listening for, a boat rubbing against the pier. Tanner's men were getting ready. They had stepped off the deck onto the pier.

Renata stopped abruptly. She made a few quick steps foward, taking her into the center of the finger of the pier where the *Spring Tide* was tied. For a second she paused there, then spun, and began to run back the way she had come, staying close to the open edge of the wharf.

She heard a curse, and the sound of running feet. She didn't look back. There was open water at the edge of the wharf. This was the moment. With all her strength she willed it: Russell fire! Fire now!

As if at her command, the shots came. Renata counted: one, two, three. On the count of four, she staggered, spun, and fell over the side of the wharf into the dark, open waters below.

18

Suddenly the sound of running feet rico-
cheted off walls and echoed across black
water. A voice called, "Police. Halt or I'll
fire!" Another voice said, "Drop your weapon
and come out with your hands up."

The two men at the edge of the wharf spun,
fired in the direction of the sound of running
feet, and then, together, jumped off the wharf
into the dark waters below.

On the wharf's edge, the two detectives
stopped abruptly at the spot where the men
had jumped. One spoke into a radio trans-
mitter directing the polich launch standing
by to move in. A beam of light instantly began
sweeping the water in a wide arc. The detectives on the wharf saw nothing moving in the
light.

"Gone under the pier," one detective said.

"Can't see them between the fishing boats docked alongside. Get somebody down there."

"Do you suppose they got the girl?" the first detective asked.

Across the wharf against the line of buildings, Lenny picked up the revolver Russell had dropped, holding it by the tip of the barrel.

"Got the cuffs on him, Burgess?" Lenny asked.

"Yeah."

"Read him his rights. I'll go pick up Verian."

Lenny dropped the revolver into a small plastic bag and slipped the bag into his pocket.

"Here comes the captain," Burgess said. "You'd better bring Verian along. I think they've got a problem over there on the water."

Renata surfaced and swam slowly along until she read *Saffron Sea* on the stern of a schooner. She pulled herself up onto the floating dock beside her, removed the face mask, the regulator, the all-important compass with the illuminated dial, and put them down on the dock. She unbuckled the weighted belt, the air tank harness, shrugged out of it, and gently lowered the apparatus to the dock, making as little noise as possible. She drew in the line tied to her waist and the waterproof bundle she had trailed behind her as she swam, then slumped, letting the exhaustion ebb away.

She hadn't counted on Tanner's men diving in after her. It had taken a paralyzing minute to realize their intent was to escape, not to capture. The speed with which Ed's men had made their appearance she had anticipated, but the enemy in the water had forced her to hide before she could get to the cache of scuba equipment Mr. Tobias had stashed for her on the swim platform of the *Dolly McBain*, berthed opposite the *Spring Tide*.

There had been a few bad moments before Tanner's men got to the motorboat waiting under the open outer edge of the pier. They had doubtless come aboard the *Spring Tide* by that method. The outboard was surprisingly quiet even in starting, and Renata was sure they had gotten clean away even though the police launch had given pursuit.

That had been a blessing for her, having attention diverted away from herself. She had retrieved the diving gear, gotten into it, and away from the wharf before the launch returned. The swim to the yacht club underwater had been without mishap. The exhaustion was more emotional than physical. Now she must get out of her wet clothing and into the dry things in the waterproof package.

Renata stood and looked around to be sure none of the people living aboard their boats were about. The *Saffron Sea* she knew from childhood. Her owner was a Bakersfield attorney who had been her father's friend, and she had sailed on her many times. In November the boat would be laid up for the winter while the attorney and his wife went vacationing. She need not worry about them, but there was always someone who came weekly to check things out, run motors, test mooring lines, and ventilate the cabins. Oh, well, she'd be safe as long as tomorrow wasn't the day.

Renata took one more look around, then unzipped the blue canvas that covered the *Saffron Sea* completely where the two aft sections joined. The cover was tent-like where it stretched over the boom above the cockpit. She swung her diving gear on board, then taking the waterproof package with her, she hurried along to the showerhouse. If she was to use the facilities of the marina, it must be now.

Twenty minutes later Renata, showered, hair washed, and dressed in clean jeans and loose sweatshirt, returned to the *Saffron Sea*. She stepped aboard, zipped the cover closed, and in the complete darkness, took a small flashlight from her pocket. By its light she looked in the old hiding place in the lazarette, the storage space on the wheel housing, for the key. It was there. She unlocked the hatch doors and went down the companionway into the galley, then along to the owners' cabin. Renata pulled back the covers of the already made bunk. She looked into built-in drawers until she found suitable pajamas and put them on, then she stretched out under the covers and turned out the flashlight. In seconds she was sleeping peacefully.

Mike Wiley came into the Brass Lantern Cafe and went directly to the booth where Ed sat having an eight o'clock breakfast. Mike slid into the opposite banquette and motioned for coffee.

"The divers can't find her," Mike said. "They want to know if you want them to go on looking, or should they dredge the harbor?"

"We'll give it another hour," Ed said. "Did you get a report on Verian and Russell?"

Mike grinned. "Yeah. Lenny made the collar and he's staying with it. They got a report from ballistics on the empty shell casings. All blanks."

"Then we probably can't hold them," Ed said, as he spread jam on toast.

Mike's grin broadened. "Evidently Russell though he was firing live ammo. After a little friendly advice and a few suggestive comments from Lenny and Burgess, Russell confessed it was all Verian's idea and he is just an innocent victim."

"How about Verian?"

"Not saying anything. John Silas is on his way to see him, but Lenny's satisfied we can get them both on conspiracy to commit murder."

"How about Tanner's men?"

"There's been a little follow up. You know they were picked up by that motor boat at the

211

end of the pier and running without lights in the fog, the launch didn't pick them up. We have a witness who saw them come ashore up the beach near the summer cottages. Three men got out, and they pushed the boat back into the surf. Our fellows have picked it up. Our witness thinks they got a ride in a car. He heard one start soon after the men walked across the beach and disappeared."

"How reliable is the witness?"

Mike shrugged. "A drifter sleeping off a drunk. We were lucky we found him before he moved on."

"Have some breakfast," Ed said. "I'll go call off the divers. Then I think I'll take a cruise around the yacht harbor."

At noon, Ed met Detective Sergeants Mike Wiley and Spider Smith at the Sandpiper Grill near the yacht club. Spider was a maverick, a loner, a man who liked to work his own way. His beat, by his choice, was the waterfront. Anything that happened between the bluffs of Promenade Park, around the arc of Refugio Bay to the headland beyond the wharf, eventually came to Spider's attention.

Spider's usual lunching spots were the Brass Lantern or the Flower Drum Restaurant, but he slid into the booth sitting opposite Ed, with an easy familiarity. Just tall enough to pass academy requirements, Spider's gaunt thinness added seeming inches to his height. The long planes of his face had a sunken contour. His skin was sallow; his eyes were the color of coffee with cream, even the whites had a yellowish cast. He was a sallow-yellow man dressed in funeral black.

Ed greeted Spider, but turned to Mike. "Anything on Tanner's men?"

"No, sir."

"How about Tanner himself?"

"He's at the old family place in Montecito with a couple of men who are supposed to be clients interested in some business property Tanner owns. They have been with a real estate agent and the present tenants of the property most of today. Last night they had dinner at Tanner's place. The servants say no one left the place last night."

"You put a couple of men on it, I suppose."

"Yes, sir, but it's a big place with lots of frontage and no way to watch the back. It's going to be tough."

"How about electronic surveillance?" Ed asked.

"We got court permission, but the boys haven't found a way to get inside, and they're not picking up anything from outside."

Ed shrugged and turned to Spider. "What do you hear along the waterfront?" he asked.

"Talk about the Riff girl and Verian. Not much about Revolo. He's not known. Henry is back after spending a night at Goleta pier waiting for Renata to show. He's pretty upset, can't figure why you haven't fished her body out of the water long before now."

"Neither can I," Ed said, "if she's there."

They ordered, and discussed the divers and the tides until their meals were served.

Ed turned to Spider.

"Anything unusual going on around the yacht club marina? Anybody seen a strange boat, anybody missing a boat, any unknown people around?"

"No, sir," Spider said, "but then I haven't *asked*. Haven't spent much time at the club lately. I could talk to a couple of the boys who look after boats for absentee owners."

"Check the whole marina. Get some men on it," Ed said, "and let me know. Look into the summer cottages. See about places boarded up for the winter."

"I'm pretty sure most everything along there is occupied, Captain. Those places are popular with the crowd from the Goleta campus of the state university."

"I know, but check it."

Spider nodded and ate in silence for a moment before he said, "I'll speak to Chin Lee at the Flower Drum. He'll know if there's a strange white girl in some back room along Harbor Boulevard. I'll get back to you before dark, if that's okay."

Ed nodded and they were silent until Ed said, "You think she made it, Mike?"

"Yes, sir."

"How?"

Mike shrugged, "The public beach most likely. It wouldn't be too far and she could have ducked under water when she saw a searchlight about to pick her up. I'd say she had a pretty good chance there."

"Where would she go from there?"

"She could have a car stashed along a side street. She did that in front of Kettleman's house."

"You think Tanner wouldn't have picked her up on her way out of town?"

"Well, Captain, it must have been twenty minutes minimum before Tanner's boys got to a phone, another ten or fifteen before he got things in motion. She would have a head start. Or she could be holed up in town somewhere waiting for things to quiet down."

"Not that," Ed said. "She must get away now, or it's just a matter of time."

Spider said, "Is she a good swimmer?"

"Yes. Bart says she can play with the dolphins."

"Then she could make it to the marina."

"She could, except that we should have picked her up before she got there."

"You think she's hiding, Captain, and is going to try again to get away using the *Spring Tide*. Tonight?"

"She has no other choice now."

"Well, Captain," Spider said, "let's say you're right. Let's say she's hiding aboard some yacht laid up for winter. How is she going to get back? Say surprise and confusion worked for her going. She won't have that a second time. All you have to do is watch the water and pick her up."

"That would work, Captain," Mike said. "We can control the water."

Ed shrugged and nodded. "Okay. Cover the water. Get help from the county if you need it."

Ed listened to the two detectives talk over their plans.

"Dammit," Ed said, "it doesn't add up. If we pick her up she loses everything. All we can do is see her safely out of the country—and into Tanner's network. She wouldn't last a week.

Ed shook his head as he pushed food around his plate. "We're missing something. Something right under our noses."

19

The wind began to blow about mid-afternoon. Ed stood at his office window and watched a trawler making slow headway against heavy gusts and choppy seas.

He had worried the Riff case until his mind rebelled.

The trawler passed the channel buoy and turned toward the harbor, the seas on his quarter. Ed saw white spray fly. Gulls were doing aerial acrobatics riding the thermals off Promentory Point.

What was it he had missed?

It was getting colder as the sun dropped into the lowest quadrant.

The phone rang. Jamie said, "I'm in town. Will you buy my dinner?"

Would he! "You bet," he said, and felt a shift in his thoughts. "Better still, take pot luck with me. I'll call and tell Suzanna to put on another plate."

"That would be an imposition on such short notice."

Suzanna will love it. She's very curious about the lady who lives on the mountain. This is a miracle, Jamie. You're just what I need. This damn Riff case has me stumped. I need to talk to somebody outside about it. You're perfect. I'll tell you how to get to the house and meet you as soon as I can."

Ed gave her instructions and when he hung up, called Mike into the office.

"What's the latest on Tanner?"

"Still in Montecito. We can't pick up anything from the house, it's too far from the street, behind too much shrubbery, and there's always a radio or TV on. We have a legal tap on the phone lines, but so far everything seems legit."

"Does he stay in, or come and go?"

"He goes—to public places. He's seen with people, some we know, some we don't. It's easy for him, Captain. We just can't cover everything."

"The two men with him?"

"Gone."

"Okay," Ed said. "Don't sweat it, just don't lose him. If he's here, she's here. Where is Bart?"

"He's been out on the Boston whaler all afternoon, diving, drifting with the tide in spite of the chop. He thinks she's dead."

"Better keep track of him," Ed said.

"Heard from Spider?"

"He checked in. He's on his way."

They waited ten minutes before Spider came into Ed's office carrying a cup of coffee.

"Getting cold out there," Spider said, and sat in the chair opposite Ed.

"Find anything interesting?"

"No, sir. Nothing to put your hopes on," Spider took time to drink his coffee, before going on. "Two deputies and I have been on every boat, big and small, in the yacht club marina, Captain. She isn't there. None of the watchmen or the fellows who service boats laid up for the winter noticed evidence of anyone on board."

Mike said, "Nothing on the wharf. The fishing boats have been out and in, we've searched them going and coming. She must have gotten away, Captain."

Ed sighed. "All right. If we don't find her tonight, we call off the search, but tonight I want everything tied down. The yacht club sealed off . . ."

Spider grinned. "A tadpole couldn't swim out of the marina tonight without us knowing it."

"I want men on the wharf."

"I'm taking that, Captain," Spider said.

"I've got Tanner's men spotted, at least some of them. We can pick them up in a moment's notice."

"How about somebody on the *Spring Tide*?" Ed asked.

"Yes, sir," Spider said, "that's covered."

"Well . . ." Ed let his voice trail off. "Well, can you think of anything we've missed?"

"No, sir," Mike said. "I just hope the lid isn't on too tight."

Ed laughed. "That's possible, she might like more room to maneuver, but as long as Tanner's around, the lid can't be too tight."

Out of the pause that followed, Ed said, "I'm having dinner at home, call me if anything turns up."

The meal was simple. Red snapper in a spicy tomato sauce served with rice and a green salad, then Suzanna's perfect flan. Suzanna gave Jamie a thorough sizing-up and Ed a nod and a smile of approval. They had after-dinner coffee and brandy in the living room where a fire of cedar wood burned.

Jamie sat opposite Ed's big chair in another of similar design, but scaled smaller. Her fair hair made a glow against the dark patterned upholstery, the lamplight and the firelight doing nice things to skin and eyes and the soft blue blouse she was wearing. Ed feasted his senses and smiled with pleasure, then filed away the picture of Jamie, kitten-contented, beside his hearth, and turned his thoughts to the Riff case.

"I want to tell you everything about the Riff case," Ed said, "and while I tell you, I would like you to put yourself in Renata's place, if you can. Will you try?"

"If it will help. Obviously you think it will." Jamie smiled and settled back more deeply into the down cushions of the club chair.

Ed outlined the case, taking his time, keeping his voice even, a little monotonous in tone, trying always to present Renata objectively. He finished with a description of Renata staggering, stumbling, falling over the side of the wharf into the dark waters below, the unsuccessful search for her body, and the evidence of the blank shell casings.

"Now," Ed said, "you know as much about Renata Riff as I do. You know she has overpaid for those few months of rebellion following her mother's remarriage. You know that to survive has taken courage and *cunning*. Tanner has told her the game is over. She knows he has blocked every conceivable avenue of escape. She has chosen to try by sea and air."

Ed took time to relight the cigar he held, "That first day in my office, she quoted George Kettleman saying I had a thing against anyone getting away with murder. Since I proved her innocent of her brother's death, I have been her fall guy. She told me about Tanner, not to protect herself, but because by choosing to move against her here, Tanner puts himself in my jurisidiction. She has exposed him. Tanner and his operations are doomed, and sooner or later she (along with all Tanner's victims) will either be free or avenged. Before Bart, it didn't matter very much to her which."

Ed blew smoke ceilingward and smiled at Jamie.

She said, "Now you want me to tell you what she's done, is that it?"

"Yes."

"I'm not sure I can, or that I should try. It's really a matter of life and death for her, because if Tanner gets her she will kill herself—I would."

"I realize that. I thought you would be perceptive enough to hit on something I've missed."

Jamie put her head back and stared at the ceiling. "It is quite a puzzle. She's alive. She's hiding. She can't hide for long. She must run, and there's the pressure of time."

"She's a survivor," Ed said. "There has to be a plan within a plan . . . an escape route."

"All right," Jamie said, and sat up straight, looking at Ed intently, "I've engineered everybody to be on the wharf. I've set up Verian and Russell by giving them a chance to frame Tanner. I have you involved so you'll be there to pick up all the participants in my scheme the minute I make my run. Tanner probably won't be there, but his men will lead you to him eventually. All I have to do is take a dive and swim away." Jamie paused, thinking. "There's no other way, Ed, but to swim for it."

"*Take a dive,*" Ed said and looked into the dying fire on the hearth. "We covered the whole sweep of Refugio Bay. She didn't come out of the water onto the shore. I know she didn't."

"Perhaps, in spite of her plans, she drowned."

"Then where is the body?"

"Oh, yes, the divers." Their glances met, and Jamie gave a small smile and a shrug. "She must want you to believe her dead."

"Sure. Her death is the only thing that will stop Tanner, but she made one mistake. She substituted blanks for live ammunition. Blanks don't kill. By now, Tanner knows about the blanks."

Out of the silence that followed, Jamie spoke slowly. "She was raised here. This is her childhood home . . . there must be people she could go to for help."

"Undoubtedly, but who and how?"

He looked at Jamie steadily. What had he missed? What had Jamie said? *"All I have to do is take a dive . . ."* Dive and swim away. Of course! He had it.

Ed laughed. "Diving equipment. That's it. That's what kept eluding me. Some old friend of her father's . . . someone so much a part of the wharf nobody notices him. He stacks scuba diving equipment on the swim platform of a boat, or ties it to a piling, or some easily accessible place. She had just time enough, and the flap over Tanner's men worked for her."

Ed put his cold cigar in an ashtray and grinned at Jamie, "I'll get Mike and Spider on this right away. We'll have to find her before Tanner does."

20

Ed was patched through to Mike on the wharf and listened to his report.

"Better bring Bart in," Ed said. "They grew up together. Maybe he can help."

Ed returned to the living room to find Jamie replenishing the fire. "Will you stay?" he asked. "I've no idea how long I'll be gone. Hours, anyway."

"Will you call and tell me what happens?"

"Yes."

He went to the entry closet, got out a heavy, fully lined jacket and returned to the living room.

"Thanks, Jamie. You've been wonderful."

She smiled, cool and serene and so lovely there beside his hearth. He wanted her there always. Ed put on the jacket and buttoned it over the taupe vest. It would be cold outside, he'd better get gloves. He wouldn't kiss her now, Ed thought, he would save it all for when he came home—home to a woman. He couldn't keep back a grin at so satisfying an idea.

"You're very lovely," he said, turned and left the room. It was five mintues past nine.

Renata opened a can of sardines and looked at them in disgust. The galley of the *Saffron Sea* was poorly stocked. Sardines and crackers, canned fruit and milk. Everything else needed cooking or some sort of preparation. Well, she wouldn't starve, and she would be gone in an hour—not more than two.

Things hadn't gone exactly as she had planned. Ed's men had been all over the yacht club. She had been forced to improvise. Luckily voices carried well across water and she had been warned about the search soon enough to bundle up her things and get off the *Saffron Sea*.

Luck had stayed with her and she had been able to "borrow" a dingy tied alongside a K-36 that had a small outboard motor in place. She had kept off shore until the wind drove her behind the shelter of the yacht club breakwater. It had been enough.

Renata had not worried about being recognized. The wig, brown and cut short, in Mr. Tobias's package, along with dark glasses and loose sweatshirt, effectively turned her into a boy at a distance.

Renata sat down at the galley table and ate by the feeble light of the small flashlight. Something must have gone wrong, or she had made a mistake. Ed should know she needed room to maneuver, but the whole yacht harbor was alive with his men. Talk of her was everywhere. She had blown it.

The problem must be Tanner—had to be. Otherwise, Ed would be only too happy to let her escape. There was no help for it, not at this eleventh hour. She ate her sardines and crackers. Fortunately there was bottled water.

Nine o'clock. Time to get ready.

At ten minutes after nine, Renata unzipped a few inches of the *Saffron Sea*'s canvas cover and looked out. The floating dock between the *Saffron Sea* and the *Cricket* which shared it, was deserted. There was only one person in her line of vision, a young blonde on the deck of a small sailboat was struggling to tie up a full plastic trashbag. Renata ran the zipper its full length, waited, listening. There were people noises and sounds caused by the wind, but the wind was a help. It kept the boat live-aboards in their cabins.

Quickly, Renata swung her scuba gear onto the dock, stepped off the *Saffron Sea* and zipped the cover shut. At nine-twenty she had tied her waterproof bundle to her waist, buckled on her air tanks, and weighted belt, adjusted her face mask and regulator and slipped into the water, hardly causing a ripple.

Renata checked the luminous dial of her wrist compass and set a heading for 276 degrees. Swimming would be easy within the shelter of the breakwater, but beyond that, with the choppy seas, it wouldn't be so pleasant, but the *Dolly McBain* would be waiting. The *Dolly* was the sister ship to the *Spring Tide*. Henry had checked her out, she could handle the boat, and Henry had unwittingly told her where Ace McBain hid the keys.

Renata swam to the center of the channel and surfaced. A row of small boats almost touching each other were strung out from the end of the breakwater to the beach. Ed intended to pick her up. Something was definitely wrong. Should she go back to the *Saffron Sea* and wait for another day? No. It was tonight or never, so tonight it was.

Renata pulled in the waterproof package, hugged it to her, and sank down until she touched bottom. If the watchers in the boats were looking for a surface swimmer she would make it. Otherwise, she could only hope luck would stay with her and her compass course would lead her beneath a boat big enough to hide her air bubbles— something about the size of the patrol launch.

Spider Smith made his voice check with his six men stationed along the wharf and on board the *Spring Tide* and slid the radio back into its case on his belt. He wasn't satisfied.

In the beginning he had felt that, for once, the captain was emotionally involved in a case and overreacting. At a quarter to nine, standing in the lee of a stack of fish boxes outside Benny's fish shack, he had to agree there was something riding the wind besides salt spray.

Spider's palms itched. He felt a creeping sensation along his spine. He wished he had been in on this thing from the beginning. It was hard to get the feel of a case without knowing all the principals.

A movement down by the railroad spur caught his attention. He pulled out the radio and said, "Hiram?" into the speaker.

"Yeah, Spider. It's okay. It's Alex looking for a spot out of the wind to finish off his bottle. I sent him on."

There was always the unforseeables, Spider thought. The little people. The little things. Alex . . . It was too early for Alex. The wind maybe. Maybe . . . It was out of pattern. He didn't like it. A cardboard box further on moved, the wind bounced it from its stack, sent it scraping along the wharf.

Nine-thirty. Spider made another voice check. Fishing boats berthed along the two fingers of pier creaked and moaned as their fenders ground against the pilings. Rigging rattled and snapped. Spider had the fidgets.

At nine-thirty Ed let his car roll to a stop against the curb near Gil's Bar. He was heading the wrong way. Moments later, Mike opened the door on the passenger's side and slid in.

"Nothing stirring, Captain. We can't find Bart. His folks say he's out with the whaler, but the whaler is in the marina where it's supposed to be."

"Sergeant Wiley," came over the radio.

"Yeah, Carl."

"Bart Cameron's pickup is in the parking lot behind the Flower Drug. He must have come in from Reyes Street."

"Okay, Carl," Mike thought a moment. "You'd better stay put. I'll find him, and thanks."

"Forget Bart," Ed said. "We'll have to hope he has sense enough to stay out of the way. Get Spider. I'll talk to him."

Spider responded to Mike's call and Ed asked, "What's going down, Spider?"

"Damned if I know, Captain, but I'm glad you're here. What's your location?"

"Just west of Gil's Bar. Everything check out?"

"As of nine-thirty. If she's using scuba diving equipment, she'll probably come with the tide, and that's running near the full."

"Any strangers?"

"Alex came through the railroad spur at nine-fifteen. Early for him. Hiram sent him back."

"Everybody answer to the nine-thirty voice check?"

"Yes, sir. Even so, something's going down,

229

Captain. I'm not that itchy for nothing."

"Okay. We'll check back in ten minutes."

Renata checked her compass. The needle glowed right on course. She should be there. The turbulent water had her feeling queasy, but she would make it. Time to come up to about six feet. She kicked slowly. There, that deeper shadow. Ah, a rudder. Time to surface.

A moment on the surface, and she removed the regulator from her mouth. The name on the stern was the *Neptune*, only one berth off. A few easy kicks and there was the swim platform of the *Dolly McBain*.. Renata pulled herself up and sat for a moment letting the queasiness subside. She pulled in the package, then began taking off her gear. She had made it. The tricky part would be slipping the dock lines. A matter of seconds if everything went right. It would have to. She had come this far.

Renata gathered together her gear and stood. She swung the air tank and harness over the stern, followed it with the package, the regulator and mask, and climbed the hanging rope ladder. The *Dolly* moved beneath her, as she rubbed against the pier, rose and fell. Renata breathed in, and lifted her arms to squeeze the water from her hair.

What was that smell? Panic rose in her throat like gorge. She could feel her eyes spread wide and her mouth open to scream.

The two figures came from nowhere. One

grabbed her arms, the other clapped a cloth over her mouth and nose.

Chloroform!

How had he known? How had they gotten here? The same way she had.

Tanner would remember the *Saffron Sea*. He would remember the *Dolly McBain* was sister to the *Spring Tide*. But how . . ."

The blonde with the trash. The blonde!

Renata strained away from the chloroform. She kicked against the man holding her. She writhed. She kicked, the kick missing, her leg swinging in an endless arc. Her body twisted, floating down . . . down. . . .

The blonde. It was her last conscious thought.

It was nine-fifty and Spider was fighting a need for action. Voice check was at ten. He didn't care. He wanted to know.

"Hiram?"

No answer.

"Hiram?"

No answer.

"Kelly?"

No answer.

"Charley?"

No answer.

Hiram was at the railroad spur, Kelly at the entrance to the finger of pier where the *Spring Tide* was berthed, and Charley was on board the ship.

Spider spoke into the radio, "Captain."

"Yeah, Spider."

"Three of my men don't answer. Have Mike check all stations. It's going down."

Alex was the key. A fiver or a bottle in exchange for walking down the railroad spur. Once Hiram was located, the rest was easy. They would use a similar ploy across the street. All they needed was to clear the spur and the two key men on the wharf, but they weren't on board the *Spring Tide*. Oh yeah! Her sister ship was the *Dolly McBain*. Okay, Spider thought. Okay, he had it. He was ready.

Ed's voice came over the radio, "Spider?"

"Yes, Sir."

"The two men on the spur and Marsden's Cannery don't answer."

"They're on the *Dolly McBain*, Captain. They're coming."

They appeared in the center of the pier, one man carrying Renata. The taller man on Spider's side, the right, was holding what seemed to be a hand gun with a silencer. A stockier man carried Renata, moving with the silent swiftness of experience.

They must have taken care of Charley on board the *Spring Tide* Spider thought, leaving him no backup close enough to be effective.

They had the advantage. The spur, the pier, and his position behind the fishing boxes made a triangle, with the long baseline between his position and the spur. He must cover twice their distance in the open, and he would have to give the standard warning, backup or not.

Spider stepped from his cover, crouched low and running, "Police! Halt or I'll fire."

The gunman swung his upper torso and fired without breaking stride. The bullet split the air inches from Spider's ear.

Spider, crouched and weaving, fired. His bullet caught the gunman in the leg. Spider saw him go down, but the man carrying Renata didn't pause, didn't so much as look back.

What was wrong with her? Where was her fight? She was like a half filled sack of grain.

Spider was gaining, but the downed man was up again. Flame shot from the end of the silencer. Spider fired, and the gunman went down in the edge of the spur's canyon of black.

Spider was close enough now to get a whiff of chloroform. So that was it. He could hear running feet. They would get them!

Burdened as he was with Renata's dead weight, the man continued to move with professional efficiency through the blackness of the spur toward the street.

A bullet thwacked into a wall over Spider's head. He turned to look back. The gunman was up, but unsteady. Spider squeezed off a shot and the man went down for good.

Ed's voice called from the street. "Police. Halt or I'll fire!"

The man carrying Renata switched her so

that she became a shield for his body, and continued to run.

A man's figure suddenly sprinted from a doorway across the street and hurled itself in a flying tackle at the man carrying Renata. Hit unexpectedly, and from behind, the man's knees buckled. He dropped Renata, rolled, and came up running into the mouth of the spur.

The girl was safe. Spider fixed his attention on the running figure.

Ed and Mike began running down the center of Harbor Boulevard at the sound of Spider's first shot.

"Better get the car, Mike, we may need to give pursuit."

Mike had turned back and Ed had almost reached the spur when the man carrying Renata emerged into the lighted street. At Ed's call to halt, the man had shifted Renata so that she shielded him. Ed dared not fire.

The next instant, Ed recognized Bart as he made his flying tackle. Bart's attention was fixed on Renata. She was down, but safe.

As Ed sprinted into the railroad spur, he heard a shot fired. Spider! The fleeing man spun, stumbling, but didn't go down. A shoulder wound.

Car lights blazed into the blackness of the spur, blinding Ed. Brakes squealed. The wounded man flung himself into the open car door. The motor raced. The car roared forward, the door still open.

As Ed jumped to safety he saw Bart, Renata in his arms, impaled in the glare of the headlights.

The car rushed on with them directly in its path. Tanner would get her after all, and Bart with her! Without conscious thought, Ed fired twice, aiming for the tires. At the same instant Spider fired into the radiator.

Bart was running, staggering.

With two blown tires, the car served, the open door struck Bart a glancing blow and he went down.

There was a squeal of brakes as Tanner spun the steering wheel sending the car down Harbor Boulevard. In a matching maneuver Mike swung Ed's unmarked vehicle broadside in the street and rocked to a stop.

Tanner's crippled car, tire rubber flapping, stopped. The door on the driver's side opened and Tanner, automatic in hand, slid slowly out. He stood a moment, drawing a breath, pulling himself up tall, then he turned to face the way he had come.

"Put down your weapon," Ed called.

Tanner fired.

Ed dropped to the pavement and it was Spider's bullet that entered Tanner's heart.

Bart had simply dropped Renata when the car door hit him. She lay on her back, one arm outflung, the other across her body, knees bent. She moved, moaning. Her eyes opened. She was staring up into the nighttime sky. Where was she? She looked about, turning her head carefully. Street lights. Neon signs. She was on Harbor Boulevard. That voice . . . Ed Staple. She was safe.

There was a body beside her. The beast who had held the chloroform! Renata tried to sit up. Nausea forced her back down again. She moved her limbs. Nothing broken. This time Renata tried sitting up more cautiously. The nausea was there, but she managed. She turned to look at the man beside her and screamed, "Bart!"

Nausea forgotten, Renata was on her knees beside him. "Bart, oh dear Lord, Bart." He was lying there in such a crumbled heap. He wasn't . . . He couldn't be. . . .

She didn't hear the sound of running feet until Ed put his hand on her shoulder and said, "Don't move him, he's hurt."

"Hurt?"

"Looks like his arm and shoulder, and maybe a head wound."

"He's not dead." Renata looked up at Ed and began to cry. "I thought he was dead."

"Are you all right, Miss Riff?" Ed looked down at her anxiously. "Why don't you just stay still. We have ambulances coming."

"Ambulances?"

"Yes. They're on their way, you can hear the sirens."

"Oh, yes," Renata said in a dull, uncomprehending voice.

Even as he stood looking down at her, Ed realized reaction was setting in. The game was played out. She had won. Had his role been pawn or protector? Did it matter? How many lives had he risked? Only through luck or fate had he lost none of his men. What of Spider, for whom any death at his hand was a devastating trauma? She was free. Was that justification enough, or was freedom everything?

"Miss Riff," Ed said, and she looked up at him. His voice was low, emotionless, "Tanner Grimes is dead."

She continued to look up at him, then a strange, savage wail rose into the night. When it ended, Renata bent her head, her shoulders heaving as great sobs shook her.

Wail, Ed thought, wail and weep for all who must learn that rebellion is handmaiden to violence. He dropped a handkerchief beside her, turned abruptly, and left her there.

Ed watched the tail lights of the last ambulance disappear, then went into Gil's Bar and asked to use the phone. It was after twelve, but Jamie answered.

"You stayed."

"I had to know. Are you all right?"

"A few bruises. No men seriously hurt, and we'll be able to pick up most of Tanner's people."

"Renata?" Jamie asked.

Ed told her the facts briefly.

"So Renata is free to marry Bart and live happily ever after. I will be a while yet."

"That's okay. I know there are details,

things that must be done."

She was going to be great, Ed thought, and said, "I'll make it fast."

Ed let himself into the house by the back door. He was too weary to notice that there were no parked cars on the street. It wasn't until he was inside the still lighted living room that he knew she wasn't there.

In her place in the chair opposite him, sat the ancient reed duck decoy fashioned perhaps a thousand years ago by Indians living around Chesapeake Bay. There was a note:

Dearest Ed,

My mother is marrying again. A Christmas wedding in New York and I agreed to go. I came to tell you, but you had the Riff case to settle and it didn't seem the right time.

I'm leaving the reed decoy with you. I hope you will understand why I couldn't stay.

The note was signed, Love, Jamie. She was gone and he hadn't even kissed her.

Ed sat in his chair and stared at the decoy he had so coveted. Was it there to hold her place, or was it there as consolation.